LOON

KELVIN DANIEL

ISBN 978-1-7375827-3-1 (Paperback)

Distributed by Myscellan Books

www.myscellanbooks.com

1

LOON

Oakland, California.

Consumed in his thoughts, Loon slidin' down I-580 almost missed the exit for 98th avenue, heading home. He quickly swerved to the right to exit and bent a sharp right. He was smooth cruisin' 20 mph with the windows down and Keak Da Sneak slappin' through the car's stereo but he was barely listening to it; thousands of thoughts rushing through his mind. Living all the way up in the hills of East Oakland, a beautiful architectural view of the city can be seen on the drive up to his condominium. It was midnight and he was just coming back from a business meeting with his nephew. He carefully parked his fully loaded, black-on-black 2017 Chevrolet Silverado truck, he nicknamed the Murda Chevy in the underground parking lot of his complex beside the rows of Bentley, Porsche, Maserati, Lexus, Mercedes, and BMW's all parked around casually. Loon loved his truck;

it was nice enough for him to enjoy the fruits of his grind and low-profile enough for him to stay under the radar—which is just what he needed. Only a small circle of the inner circle knew about his main crib. There's an apartment on 85th he rarely uses and as far as the streets knew that's where he laid his head every night. Loon glanced down at the blood drying up on his white shirt and grimaced, nearly getting sick with anxiety. He wore his jacket to hide the stains and managed to get out the car.

Walking up the lobby that leads to the elevator corridor, he heard someone call his name. He stopped and glanced back. A short Filipino woman with delicate features was walking towards him, beaming. It was his fine ass neighbor, Fiona; always dressed in the loudest of outfits as if she wanted guaranteed attention. Perhaps she did and that's why she always flirted with the men in the building, Loon the most. Her husband seems to never be home. At least the husband she keeps saying she has. Neither Loon nor anyone in the entire building has ever seen him. Whenever Loon asked, she'd say, *"he's away on business."*

"Hey handsome," she said, making the goo-goo eyes she always made when she sees him. Fiona never missed a chance to show Loon she was interested, and quite frankly, he would have gladly given her the dick months ago, but he is a changed man now and doing his best to stay faithful to his fiancée Jessica. His lips twisted into a lopsided smile. "How you doing, Fiona?"

She rolled her eyes and flipped her hair attractively. "Fairly good."

Loon wrinkled his brows. "What do you mean 'fairly'?" He asked and turned to continue walking. She walked to catch up with him.

"Aside from you being the cause of that, acting like you don't want this. The second reason I can think of is my stupid boss has been overworking my ass all week."

They stepped into the elevator and the doors closed. "I thought you were a cam model or something like that," said Loon.

She laughed girlishly and playfully slapped his arm. "I do, silly but my main job is with a Graphic Design Company. I told you that."

"Oh. Sorry, forgot," he said sheepishly. Fiona barely cackled and the elevator door opened, she stepped out.

"Well, Mr. Johnson... I'm going to head to my place and endure hours of hearing everyone's blissful moaning sounds. I mean, I wouldn't even mind a threesome," she said. "Just saying, Jess is a bad bitch," she added with a shrug and made a turn to her apartment's door.

Loon grinned lazily. "Goodnight, Fiona."

"Goodnight, handsome," her voice sounded further as the elevator doors closed again.

Once the elevator came to a stop, Loon got out and did the combination to his apartment door. He stepped inside the crib; a blast of air-conditioned cool air streamed past him. The apartment was welcoming from the open door. Upon the walls rested expensive paintings and portraits of black artists. The inside of the apartment was straight perfection, modern building in the newer areas. Each curve and flaw render it flawless. Flowers were stacked in every corner and the furniture ranged from either pinks, whites, or sea blues. The interior was designed with love, that's for damn sure and everything about it screams, 'FEMININE'. There was no obvious sign of a male presence whatsoever. Loon clearly let his fiancée run the home front. He removed his jacket and strode through his home, past the lounge, and straight to his liquor bar to pour a glass of Hennessey. The Oakland Raider drinking glasses at the bar are probably the only evidence of a man in the public area.

Loon walked back to the lounge and sat on a white couch, using a remote he opens the curtains of the floor-to-ceiling windows to a beautiful view of the city. He took a sip of his drink and recalled what happened earlier. He had been at his nephew Cream's house in Richmond to pick up some bread and as Loon was leaving, Cream stopped him.

"Yo unc, Shay is pregnant," he told him with a wide grin.

Loon's eyes widened. "Wow, really nephew? Congratulations! I'm so happy for you."

He embraced him with a hug.

Cream chuckled. "Thanks, unc. It's crazy, man. I mean, the thought that I'm gonna be a father, it's just..." he was interrupted when a rain of bullets came through the front window of his house and instantly hit him in the side of his neck. Another one hit him in the arm. Cream propelled backwards in an awkward cartwheel and fell to the floor hard. Loon immediately got down on the floor for cover but the bullets kept raining, his heart pounded and his body heated up. He exhaled quickly as the deafening sounds of bullets ripping through the air sent a rushing chill through his body. Cream gurgled and his chest heaved slowly, blood trickling down the side of his mouth. He quickly covered Cream, his hands trembling, and felt his breath leave him.

Loon's eyes widened when he saw the blood on his body. At first, he thought it was his, but there was no wound or pain just the sticky moisture and the smell of death approaching.

He struggled to crawl through the kitchen and out the back door. Loon ran to the front ready for war, but the bullets had stopped. The shooter had already got away. "Fuck!" He cursed. Cream's crew who were just across the street came running towards him.

"Who the fuck was that?" Loon asked. He pulled out his gun on them, his eyes fiery red and his nostrils flaring. "How did you fuck niggas let that car up the block?"

"Hey uh, we was just" the voice cut off with a low grunt when Loon turned and smacked the guy with his gun, sending him down to his knees. He only glanced up with a bleeding nose, blood dripping on his jeans and running down his hand, and swore knowing not to return the violent favor; they all respected Loon.

The other guys grabbed Loon and tried to calm him.

"How the fuck did this happen?!" Loon demanded.

"No idea. We hit the driver though, I'm sure. But they still got away," said Teddy, one of Creams guys. He held Loon's arm steadily until his grip was shrugged off.

Loon barely nodded and lowered his shaky hand. He

ran back to the house to check on Cream, who looked badly hurt. He knelt beside him and applied pressure to the wound to help the bleeding. Cream's neck was oozing out blood as his arm lumped to the side. Loon could literally see the bullet stuck in his neck. Fear gripped him.

"Bring the car to the front!" He said without looking at them.

Two of the boys hurried out and came back only a few moments later. He turned to the guy he pistol-whipped and peeled out a couple hundred-dollar bills. "I'm sorry about that. Go get yourself stitched up at Highland hospital."

The air was electric, everyone on edge and still shaken from that attack. Loon could barely look at Cream, or focus on anything else except a boiling rage surging through him.

"Take him to Dr. Lou over in funk town," he ordered standing up. "Tell him I will settle the bill at our appointment next week and a huge tip will be included," he clenched Teddy's shoulder. "*If* Cream gets the proper treatment." He closed his eyes and took in a deep breath. He knew the business he was in was dangerous, he knew that. And he wanted nothing more than to fall back and get out clean, but the fear of going broke and going back to the life he sacrificed so much to get out of has always held him back. He was ballin', powerful, and respected. Which was all he ever wanted but at what cost? When you have it all and seen it all, do you stop or keep on hustlin'? He sighed and ran his hands over his long braided hair.

. . .

"Hey," he heard a sensual voice. He gulped down the last of his drank and looked up.

Jess stood on top of the stairs in a long white silk robe that topped a sexy white lingerie set, her perfect curves showing. She stood at 5'7 with deeply dark melanin skin shining in the light and a throwback Halle Berry short-cut. She gracefully began descending, effortlessly glowing. "I didn't know you were back," she said, jumping in front of him. "So, I was thinking we should go with silver candelabra for the reception. Should be finished with elegant roses, softening gypsophila, and garlands of crystal beads. I read on the internet that they enhance the glittering effect of the chandeliers above," she said, full-heartedly then noticed he wasn't even looking at her. "Er, babe. Are you even listening to me?" Silence. She walked over to him and placed a hand on his shoulder. "Babe?"

He looked up at her, a bit startled. "Hmm?"

She gasped. "Loon!" She exclaimed, looking terrified. "What?"

"Blood. On your shirt. Babe, did you hurt yourself?"

He glanced down and cursed internally, *fuck*. "No, it's just... it's someone else's blood. He had an accident but it's all good. Don't worry about it."

Having just escaped from what could have been a possible death, he got a feeling he won't be so lucky next time. Loon had made a lot of money over the years and was fortunate enough to have avoided prison. It was time to get out while he was ahead.

Jess started caressing his long braids. "So why do you look so worried then? It must be something. Just now, I was talking, but your mind wasn't even here. And look at you... a full glass of Henny?"

"I'm just exhausted, that's all."

A soft sigh escaped her lips and she let her hand rest on the side of his face, caressing with her fingers. "God didn't bring you this far just for you to quit. You got to stay on top," she said.

She loves Loon, but part of what attracted her to him was his lifestyle, and she would do anything to make sure they continue living like this—the fine restaurants, sweet rides, and luxury. She knows he wants to give up his brutal business and that he feels his soul is blemished each time someone gets hurt because of him. Jess agreed to marry Loon because she believes it will help her achieve her goal of high social status. To take his mind off the stress, she leaned in and kissed him. Loon was still at first, then he grabbed her head and deepened the kiss, wildly and demanding. She smiled mischievously. That was all she ever had to do. He disentangled their lips and dipped his head into the curve of her neck, his lips stroking the sensitive nape of her neck.

"You smell good," he murmured, continuously tracing kisses up the back of her neck.

Jess trembled at the sound of his tingling voice. With a surprising speed, he pulled her robe open and yanked it off her body then pushed her to lay down on the couch. Her breasts bounced when she hit the couch, tugging at his attention. His eyes became fixed on the fullness, enticed by the way her nipples perked up. He couldn't wait to reach out and devour her; he could take it slow, but that was off the table. He wanted it pure and raw.

Loon quickly yanked his clothes from his body and threw them on the floor. She smiled when he stood in front of her with a raging dick between his legs. The lines of muscles on his body gave off an aura of strength... and *that dick*; the length of it... the veins popping around the shaft like roots. He smirked when he saw the awe in her eyes and the way she pursed her lips.

With trembling hands, he cupped one of her round supple breasts, and with a skilled motion, he circled her nipple with the tip of his tongue which made her moan silently. A short gasp forced out of her mouth when he gently bit her nipple.

"I love that!" She moaned and caressed the back of his head.

Her breasts were firm and full, he could play with them all day. Except, he couldn't wait to get inside that heat between her legs. Loon gently pulled her legs up and over his hip, leaving her exposed to his wet fingers. She groaned, a damp heat forming between her wide open legs. His hand moved along her thighs and more shivers rushed through her body.

"Wait!" Jess said suddenly and got up from the couch to take her phone from the coffee table where she kept it. "Alexa play Summer Walker *Screwin.*" The sound of the song filled the space and she smirked. "That's more like it."

Loon tried to pull her back to the couch, but she

stopped him by motioning to wait. "No. Today, I take charge." Without waiting for him to react, she climbed on top of him and leaned in to kiss him. Slowly and gently, she guided him inside her. Moving her hips in a circular motion, she bounced and grinded on top of him. Reaching behind massaging his balls and moaning loudly. Loon couldn't help but think of what Fiona had said earlier. Jess kept thrusting him back in with a pace that stole his breath, she closed her eyes when she saw his bright brown eyes deeply gazing up at her.

Almost screaming after ten pleasurable minutes, he grabbed her waist and sat up, slapping against both their chests and bellies. Loon grabbed both of her breasts and squeezed them. She screamed, her hair falling to the side of her face. Jess looked so beautiful– it took his breath away.

Jess found herself gripping his ear and tugging at the braids curling over them. A strange animal-like noise escaped from his mouth and it only egged her on. Aggressively, they were both racing towards a critical goal.

And they were close.

Close.

Close.

And then, it happened. They released together. She fell on his body, struggling to catch her breath.

Loon's phone rang loudly and he sluggishly reached to pick it up from the floor. It was his guy, his day one, A1.

Loon jerked up from the couch and Jess looked at

him alarmed. Her lips parted and she sat up quickly, trying to reach for his arm but hesitating when he turned his back to her. She wanted to ask what was up but he was already on his feet.

"Put on some clothes. We got company coming."

2

Jess pressed the phone against her ear, taking light steps into the penthouse. The cool air brushed over her skin and her glossy lips stretched into a smile.

"I normally charge 10k for that," she said into the phone, the warm lights spilling over her beautiful face. "But I'll do it for 8k if you decide tonight." Her voice was steady and soft, and her words were confident. "You have to decide and send over the details as soon as possible," she added and before the person on the other end could respond, Jess hung up.

There was that thrill of being in control, and it got to her everything. Still, with a smile on her face, she strode over to the kitchen. Jess wore a short dress so tight it hugged her body and accentuated her shape sensually, showing off the curves of her hips and her ample tits. She saw the lustful glances from the men she'd passed before coming up—*and not just them*, she thought. It always made her smile, knowing all they could do was look and lust after her, and perhaps jack off to the thought of her, but would never be able to touch. A soft giggle escaped her lips.

The kitchen was state-of-the-art, just like everything else in the penthouse. She took out a glass from a drawer, the golden rims glistening under the light, and took a few steps over to the custom cellar off the side of the kitchen. Expensive bottles of wines were supported on fine-grained wooden stems, giving the cellar an ancient aesthetic.

Wiggling her fingers over the bottles, as if trying to cast a spell, she picked out a bottle and read the label.

"Hmm," she mumbled softly and shrugged. *A Fantome Cabernet Sauvignon. $1,800 a bottle, it'd have to do.*

Her hips swayed as she took the glass and bottle upstairs, pressing her feet lightly against the window steps. The lights came on as soon as she stepped into the large room, casting a glow over the exquisite setting. Jess set her phone down on a wireless charging pad, carefully placed the wine and glass on a table, and walked over to the wide glass windows.

This was her favorite part of the penthouse: the unobstructed view of the city; the majestic picture of a million lights dazzling on the horizon, like stars from a distance. It look pretty and it always made her feel like a goddess, having to stand so high up and watch the city.

She slowly let her hand run over her body, then slipped off her dress. Her boobs heaved free "Mmm," she moaned softly and squeezed both pairs, getting a wave of tingles when the tip of her fingers made contact with her hard nipples.

Her reflection showed on the glass, and her eyes fell on the several buildings around, lights spewing out of some of the windows. Jess hooked her thumb on the waistband of her lace panties, turned around, and slowly slipped it down her legs. Another soft moan escaped her lips when the cold air hit her pussy and aroused her. Turning around again, completely naked, she smiled at a naughty thought creeping through her mind.

What if there was someone over there in the faraway buildings using binoculars to watch her... what if the person had his dick out, tugging it furiously as they got a full view of her naked body.

A pleasurable shiver rushed through her body, exciting her. A new warmth came up between her legs and she moaned at the sweet feelings starting to swirl around her. The thought aroused her. Pushing a finger in between the soft folds of her pussy, she felt the moisture and bit her lower lip.

Her hands moved over her body, caressing her boobs and pinching her nipples. Jess moaned softly and closed her eyes, smiling proudly and loving the feeling of her smooth skin.

Her round ass let out a soft smack when she slapped her hands on them and squeezed, trailing her fingers over her own curves, then she massaged her thick thighs and moaned again. Her skin was a smooth dark chocolate without a scratch or blemish to be found. She had everything most men found attractive in a woman. She was yet to find a man who could resist her body which made Loon's cheating habit all the more baffling. She shook the thought away and focused on the pleasures arising and that intense ache throbbing in between her legs, prompting her juices to trickle out.

Strutting over to where she sat the wine, Jess poured herself a glass and sipped it. Her face lit up as the taste flowed through her body. Smiling, she went to the bathroom.

It was an all-white marble and stone creation, giving off a soft ambiance. It smelled of flowers and riches— and this always amused her because the smell of money seemed to linger around her these days.

"And now for the magical touch," she hummed to herself and played Trey Songs *Anticipation II* EP, pursing her lips as she skipped straight to one of her favorite tracks, *Inside Pt.* 2.

Jess smiled as soon as the song came on, and her face glowed. Taking another sip of her wine, she lowered herself into the warm water, letting it engulf her.

With a soft exhale, she relaxed. She touched herself while bathing, scrubbing her body tenderly and exploring every inch of it. Water spilled out of the bath when she raised one leg and hung it on the edge, moving her hand down her belly.

The warmth of the water made her pussy tingle, heightening the desire fanning through her body.

"Oh, fuck!" She moaned when she pressed her thumb on her swollen clit, shivering instantly. She closed her eyes slowly, pursing her lips, and slithered down in the bath, letting the water cover her chest. Waves splashed over the surface as she moved her hand up and down, sliding her fingers over her clit. Each motion made her tremble and moan.

She pressed harder, parting her legs and letting the pleasure of the warm water—and her fingers in between her legs—drive her to an explosive climax. Her boobs jiggled to the rhythm of her heaving breath. When she slipped lower into the water, the burning flames between her legs only seemed to grow wilder.

"Sometimes I wonder if I'm a nymphomaniac," she sighed and made slow circles in between her legs, spreading her lips and playing with her clit. "I'm gonna need something bigger."

Jess took another sip of the wine and reached for the side of the tub. Pressing her thumb on a button, a gold tray slid out and she pulled out a translucent dildo with a wall suction.

Licking her lips and stroking the length, she giggled to herself. "Or maybe I just need a good dick."

Water dripped onto the floor when she stepped out of the tub. The dildo wobbled a bit when she slapped the suction on the wall, then she bent over and backed up to it, guiding the tip with one hand.

Her legs trembled and she closed her eyes, picturing the real veiny thing. The tip parted her glistening wet lips, lubed up by her dripping juices. Then she pushed back hard, slamming it all the way into her.

Fuck, that feels so damn good!

Her breasts waved as she moved back and forth,

letting the dildo thrust into her. Jess grabbed her breasts and squeezed hard, moving her ass faster.

Her moans echoed through the bathroom and the steady *"smacking sounds"* of her ass slamming against the wall.

"Fuck!" Jess squealed. Her wet pussy clamping down as the dildo inches into her. Wave after wave of pleasure rocked her body as she shuddered and closed her eyes overwhelmed by the feeling.

After a while she pulled away from the wall, her legs numb. *That was intense*, she thought and snatched the dildo off the wall.

Her body was still hot, and her chest still heaved as she caught her breath. The dildo was coated with her sleek juices. Lifting closer to her face, she ran her tongue over it and tasted her juices.

"Mmmm..." she moaned and walked slowly back to the tub—slowly because each step sent shockwaves through her body—and slid back into the water.

The air-conditioned room was refreshing on her skin when she stepped back into the room after bathing, a large towel wrapped around her body. After standing for a few seconds to enjoy the air, Jess went to her panty drawer; a phone was hidden underneath the layers of well-arranged colorful panties. She took out the phone and powered it on.

As soon as the phone booted up, messages started

coming in. She narrowed her eyes and checked one of them before calling the number.

While it rang, Jess walked along the side of the bed and lowered herself onto it. The city was a dazzling backdrop behind her, and music still swirled around the room.

The line connected almost immediately and she put it on speaker.

"Yeah, I saw the messages. Just be a little patient already; I'm speaking to you now, aren't I?" She didn't let the person answer before continuing her words. While speaking, she applied lotion and KelDan Signature™ Almond and Jojoba body oil giving her body a smooth glimmer. She paused for a second to enjoy the smooth feel of her skin and that beautiful glow. Catching her reflection in the wide mirror, she smiled and thought about how she would make a great model.

Jess stopped to light the candles around the room, still speaking to the caller and barely giving the voice on the other end a chance to get any word in. The candles gave the room a romantic haze and filled it with the wonderful scents of fresh flowers.

From the mirrored ceilings, her reflection slid around with her every movement.

"I'm ready whenever you are," she said, glancing at the phone as if the person was right there. Her eyebrows bent and her expression became cold. "I've been hearing rumors about Loon cheating on me." Saying it aloud made her gasp in disbelief. She couldn't believe he would cheat on someone like her.

"The thought of it is fucking insulting," she scoffed.

"He has something everyone wants, a jewel like me, and he thinks he can just swing his dick around uncontrollably? I'm not going to take that. It's crazy because I'm the reason his businesses have tripled in profit. I'm *the* good luck charm," she continued and paused, a wry smile on her face. "It ain't even luck. I upgraded his status in the streets and this is the thanks I get?"

Jess took a deep breath, her hands clenched as she exhaled. "I don't care. I'm gonna stick it out with him but if he keeps playing games with me," her voice became hard before she let out a dry laugh and continued. "I'll leave his ass and take everything."

A short silence followed as those last words echoed through.

Finally, the voice on the other end came in uninterrupted. It was a male voice, bold and almost impatient.

"You need to stick to the plan and stop tripping."

She pursed her lips and rolled her eyes.

The voice softened, "Trust me, I can do better for you than Loon can."

Jess' eyes sparkled with curiosity when she sat next to the phone. She hesitated a bit before asking, "Why you never liked Loon?"

A scoff on the other end and the voice responded. "Loon thinks he's bigger than what he is. Since he can't humble himself, I'ma do it for him."

The spite was hard to miss.

"But why does what he thinks of himself bother you so much?"

"Forget all that," the voice cut in, irritated. "So, when you finally gonna let me hit it?"

"Well, if this boy keeps playing, it'd be sooner than you think," she jokingly said.

Her phone notification let out a soft ping just as the voice was about to respond.

He's close to the house, her phone notified.

"I have to go, Loon is coming."

"Yeah, sure. Hey, how about you send me a pic, huh?"

Jess laughed and responded with a curt 'no'.

She ended the call before he could reply and finished up her bath routine. She walked into the large walk-in closet, sorted through her seemingly endless choices of lounging robes. With a smile, she chose a white silk robe, running her fingers over the fabric; it always felt like a soft kiss on her skin.

After putting on the robe, she smiled at the sight of her nipples poking through the fabric. It felt so sexy, so she decided to snap a pic and send it, after all. These babies aren't just meant for my eyes only.

The elevator doors to the penthouse hummed and pulled her attention. Waiting a few seconds for the screen to go blank after powering it off, she tucked it away back in her panty drawer and walked out the room to welcome Loon.

3

Loon thought to jump in the shower real quick but there wasn't enough time. The front desk called, his crew was pulling up hot. He quickly threw on a simple white Ralph Lauren t-shirt and a pair of Golden State Warriors basketball shorts. Hurried and went back down to the lounge area. The door opened and A1 rushed in, followed by Grim and Lo. They looked tensed and restless.

Grim and Lo sat on the couch, A1 kept standing. He shook his head at Loon and sighed. "We were hit, Loon. They got it all big dawg. We must have been followed on the low for weeks cause we switched routes daily. We lost everything and none of the guys saw anything."

Loon felt his throat go dry as he struggled to maintain his balance. His eyes narrowed and his breath became rushed. His knuckles popped when he clenched his fists, then he growled and trashed the liquor bar. Bottles smashed against the wall and floor, staining the surfaces.

The shards crunched under his shoes as he reached for a bottle and tossed it across the room.

His crew stepped back in fear of catching fade of his wrath, and not one uttered a word—you could get a nasty blow if you made a sound while he raged out, and that was an unspoken truth among them.

He closed his eyes and took in a deep breath. *Smooth thoughts... happy thoughts... a cloudless sky.* He repeated those words in his head until his anger slowly abated, thanks to the anger management classes he'd been attending.

"Be cool," he muttered to himself and finally opened his eyes after a quiet minute. A trickling sound came from the liquor bar, one of the broken bottles spilling its contents.

He looked at A1. "Was anyone hurt?" He asked.

"Tone and Jimmy, but they'll live," said A1.

Loon tightened his lips and restlessly put his hands in his hair, he was wondering if the two had anything to do with the bust. As if he had read his mind, A1 shook his head. "I doubt that bro, it's clear they put up a helluva fight. Tone was stabbed up pretty bad and Jimmy was knocked out and ended up with a dislocated shoulder."

Loon's anger reemerged as he yelled and threw a flower vase that stood on the center table and then used his leg to kick the table which fell with a crack and shattered into pieces. "Fuck!" He cursed, panting. He wanted to lose his mind but kept himself in check. The spot was an old abandoned sausage factory down in West Oakland. That was where he stashed his drugs and money inside a huge safe he had built in there. He also had a hidden room that led in from the walls, where he and his crew use to lay low whenever things got real. Everything about the place was carefully crafted and no one ever suspected it. Someone was onto him, and that person might be the one who shot Cream earlier today.

Jessica, who heard the commotion, came down the stairs with a fast pace, a gun looking like a cannon in her freshly manicured petite hand. Loon's mouth and eyes opened, totally dazed. She raised the gun at them as she scanned the room with concentrated eyes, she had put her robe loosely back on. The boys quickly stood and raised their hands in the air hoping she can see they posed no threat.

"Holy shit!" Grim exclaimed, realizing who their assailant was.

Lo chuckled. "Damn it! My bitch wouldn't even use a broom in my defense."

A1 nodded with a smile. "Yeah, Loony's got a real one."

Jessica slowly lowered her gun. "Sorry guys, I thought I heard..." she stopped mid-sentence and gasped. "Loony! Baby! That vase was from the Wright's auction last summer. You destroyed it," she laid the gun down on the couch and rushed to where the broken parts of the vase laid on the floor.

She then turned to them. "What's the problem anyway?"

Before they could say anything, her eyes fell on their feet and she almost screeched. "Seriously?"

"What?" A1 asked.

"Get off my damn rug with your dirty ass shoes!" she practically shoved them away. "What's y'all's problem? This is an Australian Sheepskin rug, you niggas ruining."

Loon's landline began to ring and Jessica walks over to answer it. Loon noticed Lo ogling Jessica's ass as she walked away but didn't comment. Lo moved his eyes and caught Loon watching him. The hardness in Loon's eyes were hard to miss, Lo's eyes twitched as he tried to glance away. He frowned and lowered his gaze, apologizing without saying anything.

A1 picked up on the stare down and shook his head. Lo had fucked up and he knew it— he was certain Lo also knew it because of the hilarious fear creeping into the guy's eyes.

"Lo, go get the car ready," A1 ordered and Lo sighed and scurried off never looking more relieved in his life. That was A1's way of saving the fool's life even if it was only temporarily.

After a minute, Jessica turned around to look at Loon "That was Drea. She said we should turn on channel 2 KTVU news right now."

"Oh, God!" Grim exclaimed.

"Go put some clothes on," Loon said to Jess. "Do it before I end up having to shoot one of these niggas."

She shrugged and chuckled lightly. "I don't think it's necessary, babe. Dre..."

The piercing glare he was shooting her made her stop talking. She pouted. "Fine," and stopped to turn on the TV on her way. What came on made her stop dead.

Sure enough, there was a live coverage of a Police standoff with four assailants outside Mysctery night club downtown Oakland. Loon was a silent partner of that club and the four assailants worked for him. This night could not get any worse.

"The assailants have been cornered inside the club," the reporter said. *"A hostage was taken right before the armed men rushed back inside the building."*

"Oh, man! This is not good," said Grim, worriedly.

"What were they thinking?" Aı asked, looking at Loon.

Grim was soon on the phone, and Aı couldn't get a rest with his phone going off constantly—the vibration almost numbed his hand. Everyone was under tension and Loon stared hard at the news report, his mind working fast. He moved his eyes sideways when he heard Aı calling his wife and leaving messages, trying to get her to pick up or call back.

Loon didn't answer any of the commotion boiling around him. Instead, he brought his phone out and dialed one of the guys in the standoff, Chauncy. He picked it up on the second ring.

"Nigga! What the fuck is going on over there?" Loon asked without hesitation. "You're all over the news."

Chauncy cleared his throat. "Sorry, boss. We made the usual deliveries earlier, but when we were about to leave, we saw cops approaching the building."

Loon blew air out of his mouth. "Who's the hostage?"

"Some bitch, boss. James panicked and grabbed her

inside while she was walking by. I wanted to stop him, but it was too late."

"Let the bitch go, give up the standoff."

"But, boss.." Chauncy started to say.

Loon interrupted him. "I will settle the legal fees, make sure you're taken care of behind the bricks, and take care of the family. Right now, that's the only way out alive and not fucking off our whole operation."

Chauncy hesitated, but only for a moment. "Okay, boss. You right."

"Leave the line on," Loon commanded.

From the other side, he could hear Chauncy talking to James, who was also Chauncy's nephew. "Loon said we have to let her go. C'mon nephew this shits gone too far."

"That's insane. This bitch is our golden ticket out of here breathing," Loon heard James say. His voice clearly showing he was high.

"Loony gave the order. What is wrong with you?!" Chauncy yelled, irritation laced in his voice.

Loon hadn't known Chauncy that long. They met only a couple of months ago at a bar. Loon was more drunk than usual that day. Without stating what he did for a living, he opened up about wanting to change his ways with the man he met by the counter. The man had listened to Loon and they got into a long and deep conversation about philosophy and life. *"No matter what you do, the effects of your actions will stop ahead and wait for you... good or bad,"* the man had said.

That man was Chauncy. Loon always saw him as a sort of wise father and often looked to him for advice.

Loon told him how he wakes up every day risking death; how every minute of his life is literally outrunning death. It was always looming around-always waiting for a chance to strike. He went on to say he became successful in a life that was thrown upon him; a life he didn't exactly want. After talking his ears off, Chauncy gave him some encouraging advice about stepping out in faith and living his purpose.

He told him a bit about himself too. Chauncy was older and had lost his job of 26 years that day and his wife was in the middle of a battle with cancer. He stopped at the bar because he didn't know how to break the news to her when he got back home. Without his job and benefits it was going to be hard to keep up with the chemo and necessary medications she needed. His plight made Loon feel embarrassed for rambling about his issues — they were nothing compared to his.

When he tried to apologize, Chauncy laughed it off and told him not to feel that way. Loon felt comfortable enough to offer him a job. He gave him vague details of what the job entails such as pickups and deliveries.

"So, what kind of packages will I be delivering?" Chauncy asked as his curiosity mounted.

"That won't matter O.G.," Loon said indifferently, waving off the question.

"I guess," Chauncy responded and rubbed his hands together. "Just curious, you know. I guess it's not one of those uh, Amazon- deals and stuff."

Loon narrowed his eyes and became silent.

"All you need to do is drive where I say, let my people at those locations do what they do. When they are done, they'll let you know. At that point, you can leave. You either head to the next address I give you or return home. That's it. Simple."

There was no use pressing for more information, Chauncy quickly understood.

He accepted the offer instantly. Loon was like a blessing to him that day. The job was exactly what he needed at that moment.

He heard the sound of something breaking and James screeching. That brought him out of his little daydream. "You want to take her? Here, come and get her," Loon heard James say before a loud BANG sound followed suit. Loon clenched his jaw angrily which made A1 look at him, alarmed.

From the other side, Loon kept hearing aggressive sounds that indicated the two were fighting. They were arguing at the top of their lungs over the hostage, but Loon couldn't quite make out what they were shouting.

"Please let me go," he heard a tiny voice say. "Please."

Then a gunshot followed.

"James, what the fuck is your problem?!" Chauncy shouted. Loon could hear the mixed emotions in his voice – outrage and sorrow.

James didn't answer instead, Loon heard a sound of shooting which was heard simultaneously from the television. He heard Chauncy gasp, and he stood up agitated and placed his hand on his forehead. The line started to deteriorate. On the television, Loon could see the cops rushing into the building.

His second phone began to ring, pulling his attention for a second. It was Teddy, but Loon didn't bother to pick up. He didn't want to lose focus on what was going on right now. The silence and baited breaths were pulsating as everyone looked at the television, attentions hooked like a crowd eager to catch a trick, watching everything unfold like the peak of an action movie. Then there were more deafening sounds of rapid gun fire.

Loon bit on his lip hard, that night got worse.

The second phone blasted off again, and it hit Loon why Teddy was calling him. *Cream.* How could he have forgotten? There's just so much happening today.

Loon didn't want to hang up with Chauncy, so he gestured to A1 to pick up the call from Teddy.

The sounds of police yelling were coming through from the other side, it was total chaos. Loon heard a muffling sound and then a voice said, "Hey, there is a phone here. I think the line is open."

A ruffling sound came up, then heavy breathing followed before the person on the other end said, "Hello, is anyone there?" Loon hesitated for a moment, he knew that voice, but he couldn't place it and the thought bothered him. The person sighed, "Run a..." the voice trailed off and the phone was hung up.

Loon suggests the cop must have to said, run a trace, and that only made his anxiety worse. Before he could think, he heard Jess bursting out as she began to cry loudly.

Her lips quivered and her mind became filled with fearful thoughts and worries. Chauncey had been kind to her; the thought of him getting killed rattled her.

Loon glanced back with a raised brow. Her face was already getting stained from her running mascara.

Loon noticed the guys also looking really gloom. Wow. He didn't realize they were sad over this whole thing. But wait a minute...

Jess and A1 were in a whispered conversation.

"What is it?" He decided to ask.

A1 shook his head and the other two looked away. Loon tilted his head in curiosity. Yo, what's going on now?"

Jess walked over, "I'm so sorry, baby!" Jess said, crying loudly.

Jesus. Could she be any more dramatic? He almost rolled his eyes. "Thanks."

"No, you don't..." she trailed off.

Loon was getting frustrated. "What?"

"Teddy called... he... he," her face was a mess. "He said Cream didn't make it."

Loon stood there, frozen. *What was she saying? What? No. She couldn't be...*

"What?"

"I'm so sorry, babe. I am so sorry," she said, standing up before she ran to him.

The minute she hugged him, he couldn't hold it in anymore. This was just too much, even for him. He couldn't believe all that was happening and in an instant. He could already envision his life taking a bad turn.

They stood like that for several minutes and dead silence echoed throughout the entire house. They all felt the grief of Cream's loss. He was a good dude and had much love in the neighborhood.

Loon looked up after like twenty minutes.

"Babe," Jess started to say.

"We all need to get the fuck out of town," he told them, ignoring her.

"Huh?" asked Grim, baffled.

"Babe!" Jessica exclaimed with a gasp.

"The cops gotta be tracking us down right now as we speak. We gotta go," Loon said and exchanged meaningful glances with A1. Not only the cops, Meir, their supplier will literally tear him apart the moment he knows about the work that was stolen. Loon had no money to pay him back, he had been counting on this to be his last run, so he'd asked Meir to give him triple the usual amount on consignment. This wasn't the time to mourn. He will forever miss Cream and will make sure the people who killed his nephew got exactly what they deserved but right now wasn't the time.

"I swear this to you, nephew," he said under his breath.

Grim stood up. "Loon..." Grim began to say.

Loon interrupted him. "It will be fine, bruh. I'll be okay."

Grim nodded and hugged him before exiting the

condo. Loon sighed exasperatedly and slumped into the cushion feeling nauseated.

"Babe," Jess said moving forward. "Can't we just stay and put Drea on it? Drea always gets you out of crazy shit."

"Things are different this time. I don't want to get her involved, it's too dangerous," he told her.

"What about all those friends you've made over the years? Couldn't any of them help us?" She said tilting her head.

Loon shook his head at her. "Those aren't friends, they're alliances."

She pursed her lips. "Babe, you're overreacting. I don't think he will do anything. You have been partners for how long?"

"It doesn't matter, J." He said, trying to hold onto his composure. "Wouldn't help if we were family."

"Well, can't you two just talk it out? I bet he'll listen to you, and all this will be gone in a few minutes," she tapped on his shoulder affectionately. "You know you got a way with words."

Loon gritted his teeth. "Yeah. And Meir got a way with guns. Do you wanna see what happens when those two go against each other?"

She furrowed her brows. "No. But still, babe..." she was interrupted when his phone began vibrating. He took it out, cursing internally for not switching it off.

Loon stared at the incoming call on the screen, dumbfounded. It was Chauncy's number. But Chauncy shouldn't be able to call him. He was presumably dead.

Lost in his thoughts, the line ended without him picking it up. A few seconds later, a text message came in.

We coming for you, Loon it read.

"What is it?" asked A1.

Loon gave the phone to him. A1 read it and looked up at Loon, they both knew then that it was over.

Jess moved over to A1 and read the message too. She gasped, placing her hands on her mouth. "Oh, my God," she said.

Loon stood up, agitated. "Get Maria and Sadie to safety and stay with them."

Maria was A1's wife and Sadie, his 6-year-old daughter. Loon couldn't live with himself if something happened to his family because of him.

"Are you crazy? I'll get them somewhere safe and then come go with you," A1 said to him. "You know Meir will track you down, I want to be there with you when he does."

Loon gently tapped his shoulder. "Your family needs you more than I do right now, you should be there for them."

A1 nodded and hugged him tightly before he too walked out the door. Loon smiled, A1 was his oldest friend, they had always shared a unique bond, he was practically his brother.

They first met in the 5th grade after they got into a fight over a girl. A1 had caught Loon talking to Natasha, he froze at the sight and fumed inside. This was a girl he'd tried getting with for months. She was the 'it' girl in school, and she was talking to the new kid. A1 nearly went nuts when he saw the way Natasha giggled and gave Louis flirty looks, and she even let him grab her ass. That was it for him. He needed to beat Louis up, teach him a little lesson, and hopefully embarrass him in front of Natasha. The new kid was an easy target and A1 was somewhat of a bully.

Kids gathered around after school on the playground behind the dodgeball wall to watch the fight. The cheers and chants were crazy, but not as crazy as A1's rage or the calmness of the new kid.

The fight only lasted a little over two minutes, but it felt like thirty minutes as they brawled out, panting and grunting like animals. After the fight, they developed a respect for each other; the new kid was no pushover.

The scar Loon has over his eyes was from one of the blows on that day.

———

By now, Jessica was worried. She hadn't thought about Meir and what he might do to her man. Although she doesn't know how exactly terrifying Meir is, she was willing to scale it at 'really terrifying'. Still, she didn't think this has to involve her.

"Babe," she began. "Maybe you should go alone."

The look he gave her made her quickly add, "I mean, you know I'll be safe right here. They would only want you. I'm not a part of this."

Loon raised his brow as if to say, 'bitch, are you for real?' She was really testing his patience.

"Meir has always liked me, you know," she continued to say. "I don't think he would do anything to me. His problem is with you."

"And that's exactly why he will come after you; to draw me out," he sighed exasperatedly. "Meir is not a friend, J. He is not our friend. He's just a business associate."

Jess stared at him for a few seconds as if she was making up her mind.

"What do you want me to do, babe?" She asked, trying to brace herself.

Loon tightened his lips and nodded. *Better.* "Pack all the money, jewelry, and passports in one of your bags. Leave everything else. It shouldn't look like we are on the run."

Jessica nodded and jogged up the stairs. Loon followed her and went straight to his study room. Once there, he made sure he picked all the documents and contacts of people he had to warn. He sat down on an armchair and sent them all a bulk message. "Gump," he typed, which was a code for 'run'. The crew had come up with it from the famous Forrest Gump line 'Run Forrest, Run!'. The crew all knew if that word ever came through – shit hit the fan.

Jessica called out to him and he went to meet her. She was dressed in a tight fitted tracksuit, her jacket in one hand and the bag in the other, she was so beautiful. Loon gave her a quick kiss and grabbed her hand. "We're using the emergency exit," he said.

They went out stealthy as possible and walked down

the street to a nearby bar. Loon was expecting to meet someone there.

The bar was hundreds of conversations told in loud voices, competing with the R&B music that dominates the usual atmosphere. The crowd was young and mainly comprised college students. A sharp smell of vodka and the stench of cigarettes wafted towards them, like black plumes bellowing from burning woods. Then Loon saw him sitting by the counter, sipping on a drink. Feeling a bit woozy, Loon walked and sat beside him.

"Never a bad time, Kwan," he said.

Kwan turned around, grinning widely when he saw Loon.

"Loon," he said. They shake hands and Kwan nodded in greeting towards Jess.

"I got you a Henny light rocks, my good friend. What does your beaut-"

Loon pats his shoulder and chuckled. "Actually Kwan, I'm in a hurry, my friend."

Kwan arched his eyebrows. "Really, what's up?"

From the corner of his eye, Loon noticed two guys—definitely college boys—whispering at each other and checking Jessica out. He bit his bottom lip.

Be cool, he told himself. It's nothing.

They got up and walked the few feet in her direction. One of them, Asian, winked at her, and she smiled. They were talking sort of loudly, so he could hear what they are saying.

"Fuck she's hot," the other guy, a Caucasian, said. "Can we buy you a drink?"

Jess giggled. "I'm not done with this one, but sure." Even in sweatpants and hoodie, she turned heads. She liked attention and knew exactly how to use it.

He clenched his fist and then relaxed them. Loon's eyes were fixed on Jess and those guys.

When did she even get a drink? Loon thought to himself.

One of the boys had the audacity to grab her hand and she giggled again but quickly pulled away. Finally, his eyes met Loon's glare. If looks could kill, those college boys would be six feet deep.

Loon silently hoped he wouldn't have to disfigure them. He wanted to stay as low-key as possible and knocking out two guys wouldn't help with that.

They walked away when he grabbed Jess's hand and entangled it with his as she made that annoying giggle and slapped him lightly on his shoulder.

Kwan noticed Loon's expression and watched him battle to hold his anger. He thought Loon was upset with him and was eager to do anything to help.

Loon turned his attention back to Kwan. "I need your car."

"Er, what-"

Loon interrupted him. "5 bands right now for it," he said.

Kwan faltered for a moment, no doubt thinking what on earth Loon would want to do with his car when he could afford any car he wanted. He figured if he was asking for his, he must really need it.

He finally nodded. "Alright, but keep your money," he said to him.

Loon smiled. "Thank you. And in that case, you should go to my condo and tell Emilio, the garage valet, I said to give you the keys to the Maserati. Use the code word 'Halle Berry', he'll know what's up from there."

Kwan grinned widely, pleased with the exchange. He dipped his hands into his pocket and brought out the keys. "Here. Be safe," he said, offering them to Loon.

Loon took the keys and thanked Kwan again before he and Jessica stepped out of the bar into the chill of the night.

5

1 HOUR EARLIER

Walking into the Mediterranean restaurant was like stepping through a portal, and the thought amused Meir. Leaving behind the bustling mix of honks and screeches, engines and curses–the sounds of the city–the ambiance inside the restaurant felt more like a warm embrace.

Meir stopped by a few tables, shaking hands and offering warm smiles while saying hello to a few friendly faces, all immaculately dressed.

He caught sight of the hostess, Laila, up ahead and felt that stir inside him again. He made the 'hello's' quick and went over to meet her. She looked sumptuous as usual; her body invitingly sexy. It was hard to ignore the fierce need gripping him each time he caught sight of her.

If he had the chance, he'd bend her over one of those tables, hike up her skirt, peel off her panties, and fuck her good. Meir wanted to feel her body; taste her and fuck her till she screamed–the mere thought of it made his dick throb inside his pants.

"Shit!" He cursed under his breath when he felt the boner forming. He cleared his throat as he approached Laila, shifting his mind to other things before he had an embarrassing tent in his pants. It was best not to get intimate with any of his staff, and that was rule number one but this was Laila. He could feel himself getting closer to breaking each time he saw her.

There's something about her, he would always think to himself, and the thought of it was torture.

Laila was all smiles when she got to him. Her eyes had that moon-like shimmer, and it bugged Meir because he didn't like to think of himself as poetic.

Focus! He snapped at himself when he saw her lips moving.

"We've had a steady flow of customers all day so far," her voice came into focus.

"I can see that," he said, looking at the buzzing activities around him. "It's amazing."

She blushed.

Fuck, he thought. *If only I could pull her into one of the back rooms.*

Meir tried to keep his eyes on her face—and not on those curves—as he informed her that table six was on the house.

"Whatever they're having, I'll take care of it."

She noted it, as efficiently as always.

"Good." He caught a subtle bounce of her boobs and his heart lurched. He'd need a good fuck soon, if not his dick would rip through his pants. That was certain.

She was speaking again.

"Your office was locked again so I couldn't drop last night's deposit in the safe," she informed him. "I left it in my locker. I could go get it now." Her voice swayed beautifully and she held his gaze perfectly.

"That's okay. Hell, I'll get it from you later. Ain't a problem."

If his office was locked, Lyor must have snuck in through the back. That only happened when they had to make a move, or when they snuck someone in to brutalize them for information. The screams would always be muffled, but that couldn't be said about the beating. He couldn't wait another minute to see what was going on, even though he'd have preferred to see Laila's smile all evening-or tap her ass or pin her against a wall and fuck her hard.

Focus, dammit! He sighed.

"Keep up the good work," he said and touched Laila's arm before leaving. That short touch made him realize he just might not be able to control himself much longer around her.

He got into business mode when he crossed the hallway and went into his office, leaving the sounds behind him.

The heavy grunts of a man in pain greeted him as soon as he entered.

Lyor was there alright, sleeves folded up and a razor box cutter in his hand. Meir could tell from the hard expression on Lyor's face-the sweat on his brows, the blood on the cutter, and all that the other guy was having a bad evening. 'Private time' with Lyor certainly had to be a bad evening, no matter what.

The man hung by his arms from the exposed water pipes above them.

Lyor's voice tore angrily through the air. "Where the fuck is our missing product?!"

The hanging man had his head down, groaning softly. The pipes creaked as he swayed, his arms were sweaty and strained, and his body riddled with cuts.

The man heaved and looked up slowly. "I... I don't know."

"Wrong answer!" Lyor growled, squeezing his grip on the razor box cutter, and sliced the man's side, cutting into his flesh and drawing a trickle of blood. "You better tell me the truth soon or you'll bleed out," Lyor warned.

Red dots covered the floor under the hanging man, increasing with each cut.

"That's enough," Meir interrupted, sure that Lyor would finish this guy before he had the chance to find out what was happening. Before he could ask for more details, the breaking news flashing on the mounted TV caught his attention.

A reporter rolled out the news quite succinctly, while words scrolled along the bottom of the screen.

"Multiple gunshots have been reported in the ongoing Police standoff against four assailants outside Mysctery night club, downtown Oakland..."

Meir narrowed his eyes and cursed lightly. He wouldn't have cared about it on a normal night, except he knew that nightclub and a quick zoom from a helicopter hovering around the building confirmed what he suspected; it was one of Loon's spots.

The reporter's voice went on.

"...sources say the nightclub has been under investigation for some time now, on suspicion of drug distribution and money laundering."

Lyor's eyes were on the screen now, and the grim expression on his face softened a bit.

Both men walked closer to the TV to get a better view of the news, leaving the other guy hanging. Meir folded his arms and watched the news with rapt attention, and Lyor shook his head slowly.

"I don't like this," he muttered and turned to Meir. "This might be a problem for us as well, you know; Loon still owes you 2 million for the shipment you just gave him a couple days ago. If the feds are closing in on him, I guess we can kiss that money goodbye."

Meir snarled and gritted his teeth, his nostrils flaring and his eyes sparked. His mind worked fast while he kept his eyes fixed on the flashing images on the screen.

A soft ache of his knuckles made him unclench his fist. He turned to Lyor and snapped his fingers.

"Get Loon on the phone now."

"On it," Lyor said and took out a phone.

He took a step away and dialed Loon. His face folded when the line beeped without any response. A soft curse and he dialed again. Same thing; no response. "He's not answering," Lyor announced in a hard voice that caused Meir to grit his teeth.

It wasn't in Loon's character; he always picked up for Lyor in respect to Meir, so this was certainly strange.

It probably had something to do with that breaking news and there was only one way to find out.

"Let's stop by Loon's condo for a surprise visit."

Lyor nodded and grabbed his jacket. They headed for the door when Lyor stopped and jerked his thumb in the direction of the guy hanging.

"What about that fool?"

Meir turned around coolly. "How much did he steal?"

"Sixty grand," Lyor responded, his eyes hot on the guy almost as if he wanted to rip into him.

Meir waved his hand and grunted as if irritated by the sum. "Just leave him, we've got bigger worries."

Lyor's gaze on the man was bloody and chill-inducing, the man stared with swollen eyes and quivering lips, half-expecting to get shot in the gut.

They turned around once again and continued leaving.

The man gasped and shook his head, pulling his weight against the creaking pipes. "Hey... hey! You can't just leave me like this!" He screamed.

His arms were already numb, and he was certain he'd never survive the hour.

Lyor opened the door and Meir walked out. The man's screams bellowed after them, but as soon as Lyor stepped out and closed the door, the sounds ceased. And for good reason; Meir had the office soundproofed a month ago after he'd had to kill one of his top employees because she overheard Lyor torturing another guy.

Meir cursed a lot that day, knowing there was no way he could let the trembling woman live after what she heard. It stabbed at his heart when he saw that chill in her eyes, he heard the way her voice shook when she begged him. That couldn't happen again.

"And you better take it easy with the whole torture stuff, it's almost as if you fucking get off on it," he'd snapped causing Lyor to grin.

Lyor turned up the brute again when they arrived at Loon's condo.

"I'm sorry but I cannot let you in," the front desk clerk repeated, a bit uneasy in the presence of the two.

"We won't repeat that request a third time," Lyor threatened with a sneer. "Unless you want that skinny arm twisted off." He then turned to Meir and said, "Please let me boss. I'll snap his shit quick."

"No, please don't," the clerk whimpered. Something about Lyor's gaze made the young clerk know the man was serious.

Meir grunted his impatience and tossed a couple thousand at the clerk. Several thoughts rushed through his mind during the elevator ride up to the penthouse, and Lyor's silence suggested the same.

"Something's not right here," Meir said when the elevator dinged and the doors opened.

"Yeah, no shit," Lyor whistled. "This place is a mess."

Moving around slowly, Meir took in the sights. His eyes caught the shimmer of shards of broken glass littered on the floor. The TV was still on with the same live news report they'd been watching back at the restaurant, and the volume was turned up. He could almost imagine someone sipping a drink when the news came on, then turning up the volume and jolting upright.

They fanned out and searched the penthouse.

"There's no one in here," Lyor said, meeting up with Meir in the master bedroom. "Someone was in a hurry," Meir replied, gesturing to closet doors left wide open and the few hangers scattered on the floor.

"Loon's on the run."

6

PRESENT DAY

Before he and Jessica could leave the country, Loon wanted to collect his debts, knowing undoubtedly, they'll come in handy. He drove them down to the outskirts of Oakland and parked directly in front of a shabby motel. Loon figured it will be the perfect place to lay low, they don't really ask for IDs and no one will think he'd come here. They got out of the car and entered the motel, which was even dingier on the inside. Disgusted, Jess tried hard not to stare. They approached the counter, where the manager of the motel where a plump middle-aged middle eastern man stood.

He grinned and walked up enthusiastically when he saw Loon and Jessica, looking eager to welcome people of their standards into his stinking lodge. Loon could tell it hardly ever happened.

But surprisingly enough, that wasn't the only reason he got all excited. "Whoa, whoa! Pretty girl, where'd you get her, amigo?" He asked smiling, showing a set of yellow-stained teeth.

He checked Jessica out again and gasped as if he couldn't believe her structure and physique, then he winked at her and licked his lips.

Loon was about to lose it when he figured the manager was probably used to seeing prostitutes; that was literally what this place was for. Jessica frowned and opened her mouth to talk, but Loon stopped her by holding her hand in his. The man let out a croak-like chuckle and rubbed his sweaty hand over his bald head before extending it to Loon.

He grimaced and stared at the sweaty fingers. The man got the idea and instead wiped his hand on his dirty shirt. Loon grunted and caught a broken wall clock, wondering if they could get a better place. Apparently, Jess was still all twisted about his comment earlier.

She didn't yield. "What the fuck did you just say?!" She shouted. "Who do you think?"

Loon squeezed her shoulder and whispered, "Come on. Lay low, remember?"

Usually, she loved when men drool over her, but he guessed she found this particular compliment offensive and disrespectful.

The guy was looking really confused.

"Hahaha," Loon laughed it off. "Yes, yes. My friend Pimpy Dough hooked us up. Only the best."

The manager laughed even harder, killing off the awkwardness. "Pretty sexy."

Jessica was glaring daggers at him, but Loon ignored

her. He didn't want to draw unnecessary attention to them or make them look unfit. Besides, they were going to be out of the place soon, no reason for theatrics.

They checked in and the man gave them the keys to Room 109. Jessica snatched the keys out of his hands, infuriated. Loon smiled at him and quickly trailed behind her. The room was a tiny space with one bed, a table, and one chair. It smelled like underwear were piled in the corner that clearly haven't been cleaned out.

Jessica fringed. "Jesus!" She cried and aversely walked inside. Loon followed.

"Look at this place, babe," she said. "Look at where you brought us." She grimaced at the bed. "Ew. probably has bedbugs. I honestly don't understand why I had to come here."

Loon clenched his fist. She was starting to get on his nerves.

"Babe, look at the floor in this shit. Just how much dust can a single space acquire? And people actually stay here?" She paused to cough.

"We could've gone to a 5-star hotel and got in through the back door. Why did we have to come here? That man at the front desk literally called me a prostitute."

Loon closed his eyes. He has so much to teach her, even though he has been doing so for months. Jess was a slow learner. In fact, too slow, but she'll get there.

He realized getting pissed was not the solution at that moment. He was putting her through this, so the least he could do was be patient.

He gently touched her hair. "I'm so sorry, J. I would never intentionally put you here. But I'm sure Meir is looking everywhere for me. This is the last place he'll expect to find me, especially since he knows I'm with you. A shithole like this is not where you find real baddie like you." He added that last part with a grin.

Jess pouted for a few seconds, trying to hold back the smile forming on her lips.

"Ugh, fine. But don't think it's because of that smile on your face," she said. "I'm tired of running around the city. I just need a rest till morning, at least."

"I'm sure even this place can't fuck that up," Loon responded, giving the place a once-over.

She put her bag and jacket down on the table and began clearing out the room.

He knew Jessica was only doing this for him and he felt bad for having to put her through it. Loon could hear the chatter of some kids playing in the parking lot coming through the window. He looked out and saw three boys possibly in their early teenage years laughing at something. He stepped outside and a rotting stench filled his nose. He couldn't tell where it was coming from but damn was it foul. Loon cleared his throat and signaled to the teenager on the bike. Reluctantly, the boy walked over to him, which made his friends turn around and look.

"Hey, little fella. Do me a solid?"

The boy shrugged. "What is it?"

Loon brought some money out of his pocket. "Here's a $100 for you, I want you to ride your bike over to the

Walmart store across the street and get me... wait." He went and took a notepad out of Jessica's bag, then listed all the items he needed.

"Cool, here's the list for everything, you'll get another $100 when you come back," he said, handing him a $100 bill.

The boy nodded. "Alright."

Loon watched as the boy whispered something to his friends and then the three boys sped off. He turned to Jessica who was pulling some things out of her suitcases, looking absolutely appalled. He clenched his jaw and strode over to her. Gently, he grabbed her waist from behind and pulled her into him. He dipped his face into her neck and breathed in.

"I'm sorry," he said into her hair.

Her heart skipped a beat as he bit softly on her ear. She chuckled dryly. "It's okay," she said. They then stood like that for a while, until she broke it off.

He sat on the only chair in the room and laid his head back on the headrest. He heard her fumbling around in her bag, looking for something. The clacking sounds weren't allowing him to think like he wanted to, so he sat up and looked at her.

When their eyes met, he raised a questioning brow.

She sighed. "I have to call Aunt Winnie."

Loon groaned.

"I'm sorry, babe, but she will go cuckoo if she doesn't hear from me in a few. You know how she is," she added.

He did know how she was.

"We can't make any contact with anyone right now,

Jess. Meir will be watching out for that," he said. "It's too dangerous."

Jess nodded. "Okay," she said silently. He could literally feel the sadness in her voice.

He stood up and walked to her. "Okay," he said.

She looked up. "What?"

"Okay, you can call her."

He saw her eyes lit up.

"But not with the burners. I think I saw a pay phone next to the vending machine outside," he added. "You can use that."

She jumped up and down happily and kissed him. "Thank you, baby. I'll be quick." She ran out.

Loon sat back on the chair. A few minutes after, he heard multiple knocks on the door. The little boy stood there with two large plastic bags, and beside him, was Jess.

He smiled. "Wow, that was fast. Thanks!" He collected the bags from him and put them on the bed.

Jess walked in and helped him with collecting the bags. Loon thanked her and ruffled her hair a little bit, then he looked at the boy. "How long have you been friends with your... friends?" He asked.

"Like eight years," answered the boy.

"Good. Then you will share this money with your friends. That's what standup guys do, okay?"

Before the boy could answer, Loon felt Jessica's hand on his back. She giggled, "Let the boy go have fun, baby," she said.

The boy then blushed.

Loon leaned in and whispered to him, "Take care of your homies, boss up and one day you'll have a woman like mine." Smiling, he pushed the boy's forehead away from the door and closed it on him.

Jessica went to open the bags and her jaw dropped when she saw what Loon made the boy buy. "Babe!" She squealed out.

"What?" He asked, wide-eyed.

"It's nothing. Just... how did you know to buy all these? And you remembered my tampons. Oh, shit and you got my *Twizzlers* black licorice! That's so sweet of you, baby."

Loon never understood how she liked them nasty things but he didn't care, it made her smile.

Loon's lips twisted into a kind smile. "Just wanted to make you comfortable," he looked around the room. "As comfortable as you can be in this tiny foul ass room," he said, causing Jess to laugh girlishly. He helped her remove the sheets and pillowcases from the bed and they replaced them with the new ones the young boys had just bought from Walmart.

Loon noticed that Jess kept glancing at the door as if she was expecting the police or Meir to bust in on them at any moment.

She placed her hand on her wide hip and took in the view of the room. "There, that's better," she said, loving the look of the new sheets and pillowcases.

Loon grabbed her waist. "Know what we need now? A nice hot shower."

Instantly, he helped her remove her tracksuit. Then

he grabbed her waist again and kissed her. Jessica giggled amidst it and when he began to touch her, she playfully pushed him off.

"Come on," she said with a wink.

He reached forward and grabbed her wrist, pulling her close to him. He slapped his hand on her ass and held her tight against his body, pressing his lips on hers.

"No, you come on," he breathed and led her into the bathroom.

"What about your clothes?" She asked.

"You tell me," he answered with a grin and spanked her ass again.

She giggled and bit her lip, loving that firmness of his hand on her backside. She helped him take off his clothes, before squatting low and giving his hard dick a soft kiss before they entered the bathroom.

The bathroom however was surprisingly clean. Jessica turned on the shower and stood under it. She snickered when their eyes met. Loon moved in to kiss her, the warmth of his lips and the water made her shiver with pleasure. He kissed her gently at first, then tasted her hungrily. His hand moved along her curves, and back up to her ample breasts, squeezing hard.

"Oh god, your hands are magical," she moaned, holding his shoulders.

She felt like he had many hands, caressing her all over and many tongues, passing swiftly from one nipple to another. Then came the pressure of his fingers thrusting in and out of her, his lips against hers again. Which was exactly how she wanted it. With his other hand, he massaged her breast then pinched hard on her nipple, making her moan in his mouth. Loon then grabbed her neck and pushed her against the wall while savagely kissing her neck. Lightly smacking her face which caused her to moan even louder, thanking him after every smack.

His hand moved down her thighs until he had a firm grip on her legs. With her back pressed to the wall, he lifted her leg and jammed his dick in between her legs, grunting as he felt her warmth.

"Harder!" She gasped and clung tight, pushing herself forward as he began a steady thrust into her.

He held her face under the shower head, his hand on her throat, and fucked her with growing intensity till she trembled and panted. Jessica's voice cracked and her eyes rolled inwards. Loon continued pounding in and out of her while she shuddered through her climax until he groaned and came hard as well. Jess jumps down to put him in her mouth making sure to catch every drop.

They stood there, tangled together for a while before Loon offered to wash her up. He circled her breasts with the soap and she giggled excitedly.

He looked straight into her chocolate brown eyes. "I'm sorry for everything. Just trust me, I will fix this. Everything will be back to normal, I promise."

Jessica smiled perkily. "Hey, life is perfect... if we are together," she said and leaned in to kiss him. She then chuckled and pushed his chest back. "Now, I'm going to go make us dinner from the microwavable snacks the boy picked up."

She walked out, but Loon stayed behind to finish his shower and figure out a plan before they hit the road. He was halfway through when he heard Jessica's loud scream from the room. Pulse rising, he rushed out of the bathroom, naked and the water still running.

Meir and his goons stood inside the room, one of them had his gun in Jessica's mouth and was pulling her hair back mercilessly. The other had a knife and started to slide it all over Jess's body as if he was trying to find the perfect spot to slice open.

"Well, well, well. Look who we have here. Loon Johnson. Trying to skip town without settling with me?" Meir asked.

Loon felt sick to his stomach, frozen by the sight of Meir. The goons jumped to give Loon what they thought to be a proper beating. A hard punch crashed into the side of his face knocking him to the floor. Loon grunted when he hit the floor. Before he could take a breath, boots smashed into his ribs, hard kicks and stomps came from all over.

Jessica's screams rose above the mess, and a harsh 'shut the fuck up' followed.

"I'm gonna cut off his fucking balls, outta my way," Lyor growled and took out a knife. He pressed the tip of the blade beneath Loon's shaft, but Meir called him off still leaving a thin cut before he reluctantly backed off.

7

Meir grabbed a shirt under his feet off the floor and tossed it at Loon. "Clean yourself up."

He used his legs to push out the chair from the table and sat on it. "Seriously, Loon? I thought you had better taste than this dump," he said and laughed with his boys.

Meir smirked at Loon. "Put on some clothes, homeboy."

Loon subconsciously put the bloody shirt on, all the while keeping his eyes on the guys holding Jessica. He moved too fast reaching into his duffle bag though, and that instinctively caused Chuey, the other goon to fire a shot at him. He jumped away, but it grazed his thigh a little bit and God damn did it burn.

"Don't try anything funny, my nigga," Meir told him. "Like for instance pulling a gun out of that bag. Ya hear me?'

Loon nodded while grimacing in pain. "I won't man, damn."

"Good," grinned Meir. "Lyor, grab some pants for Mr. Johnson, would you? Make sure we could trust him."

Lyor quickly rummaged through the bag and tossed a pair of pants at Loon, who threw them on just as quickly.

Meir grinned again. "There, that's better. So, here's the thing Loon, I know you got busted. And I'm pretty sure you're going to tell me you don't have my fetti," he stood up. "But what I don't hear is, how you plan to make good on *my* 2 milli worth of guns that was jacked or your plan to pay me back because you clearly were planning to skip town without telling me."

Loon sighed helplessly. "I'll get your money, Meir... in a few days. I have a lot of people who owe me money in this city. Can you please tell him to let her go? She has nothing to do with this," he beseeched.

He knew how his line of business worked, so he occasionally would lend money to people, usually, standup street guys, whom he saw like a human savings account. He could withdraw whenever he needed to in an emergency. And now that Meir had a grip on him, *this* was an emergency.

"I was running from the feds not you, Meir," he said. "I planned on hitting you up, soon as I got situated."

Meir threw his head back and laughed hard. Loon couldn't tell whether it was in agreement, sarcasm distaste, or all three. Meir pulled out his gun and swiftly turned around to the guys holding Jess. In the wink of an eye, his gun was at the side of her head. That confirmed it wasn't in agreement. Meir obviously wasn't satisfied.

Jessica, on the other hand, was terrified and started

struggling to get free, her screams muffled by the gun in her mouth.

Lyor pulled her hair harder. "Shut the fuck up, before I make your sexy ass real ugly," Meir shouted into her ear which made her cringe with fear. Tears were rolling down her cheeks, and in that moment, Loon had never felt more enraged but this time he was going to have to sit with that anger.

"Here's what's going to happen, my friend," Meir spat. "You will come to the warehouse with my money in 24 hours, not a minute more, otherwise Lyor here puts a bullet through her gorgeous head." Lyor removed the gun from Jessica's mouth and placed it on the other side of her head, then made a shooting sound and squealed with laughter.

"Fine. I'll bring it. Just-please let her go," Loon said, overwhelmed. "Meir... Meir. Please. Remember the good business relationship we had.

Jessica spoke up, "There is... there is half a mil in the duffel bag under the bed, you can take it and leave us alone for now."

Loon clenched his jaw in aggravation. He understood that she was panicking but telling Meir about the money wasn't going to make their situation better. She didn't know that, and it was justifiable because, until yesterday, she was living a normal privileged life, having to worry only about her wedding plans, make-up, and fashion trends. Loon hated himself for what he was putting her through.

"No, Meir. You can't take that, it's all that I have to duck the feds," he said.

Meir chuckled humorlessly and nodded at Lyor, who grabbed Jessica's hair and shoved her to the floor, her head hitting the edge of the bed on the way down. "Get the bag!" He commanded.

Meir walked to Loon and placed his hand on his shoulder. "I'm going to take your bitch hostage until you pay up in full," Meir said to Loon.

"And I'll rape her repeatedly just before I put a bullet through her head," Lyor said.

Loon's eyes widened. "I swear to God if you lay a hand on her, I will kill you myself." He was trying so hard not to blow off.

Chuey tilted his head tauntingly as if he was accepting a challenge. He placed one hand on Jess's breast and one on her ass and squeezed both.

Loon barked at him. "Get your muthafuckin' hands off her!"

He didn't listen. He just kept on feeling all over her and Jess just cried. Loon gritted his teeth and breathed hard. He wanted to pounce on that fool and snap his neck, but that would only get him killed. And it scared him, the thought of what they'd do to Jess after.

"That's enough, Chuey. We not here to fulfill your perv fantasies," said Meir. He turned to Lyor, "Put her in the car."

Loon shook his head vigorously. "No, please. No! Meir, for real! Stop. You don't have to take her. She has nothing to do with any of this." But it was no use, Lyor was already dragging Jess out of the room.

"Babe!" She cried out.

Loon made sure he gave Lyor the 'I'll be seeing you soon' stare before he walked out, cause he would, and when he does, he would rip him apart.

"I'll come for you, baby. Everything will be okay, I promise!" Loon called out.

The rest of the boys followed Lyor out.

Loon's clenched fists ached now, and he needed to punch something... or someone.

"I like you, Loon. I like how you work; you were always on time with payments. I don't know what exactly happened, but you fucked up this time. Now I promise you, I take no pleasure in all this, but I will destroy you if I have to. Don't make me have to," Meir said and squeezed on Loon's shoulder rather gently, and at that moment, Loon could see it in his eyes, Meir wasn't enjoying this at all. But business was business, and in their line of business, friendship, and empathy are extinct. He knew Meir's Uncle, Ezra Kapon, was making him do this.

"Can I talk to him?" He asked.

"Who?"

"Ezra. Can I talk to him?"

Meir shook his head. "He doesn't even know about this yet. That's why we're only taking her. If he had, you know everyone you love would be dead by now. He knows where your aunts, cousins, and your square ass friends live."

Loon closed his mouth, he was speechless.

"Oh and one last thing, we've located A1. Just waiting on instruction of what to do with him."

Loon's eyes widened. "No."

Meir shrugged.

"Meir, I promise. I will make this right. I will pay up my debts but please don't touch anyone," he begged. "Please."

Meir nodded and shrugged again, "You better."

He pats him on the back and walked out of the room.

Loon was finding it hard to breathe, he put his hands in his hair and paced around the room. He then stopped and placed both of his hands on the table. "Fuck!" He yelled out angrily.

He instinctively threw the table at the wall and flipped the bed and the television, literally destroying everything in the room.

Loon's back was arched like a raging animal, and his chest heaved with each heavy breath. He scanned the room, catching the flick from the table lamp. He took a few steps over and snatched the lamp from its position, the cord snapping out of the outlet, and tossed it against the wall. His hands trembled and his eyes itched.

He couldn't see clearly, and he just doesn't seem to understand how in less than 12 hours his life had turned upside down. He was literally living in his own damn nightmare. Loon had always been careful with how he operated. Now, Cream is dead, his stash spot was hit and Jessica is at the hands of a diabolic Drug Lord. Someone was after him, but who? No one ever had the nerve of coming near him, he was powerful, he had built himself up like that and his reputation precedes him. So, who on earth was messing with him?

A knock at the motel door interrupted his thoughts, he squinted his eyes, wondering who it could be.

8

KIMBERLY

3 days ago - Atherton, California

Kimberly sat in a Lexus RX a few houses down from her house with her boyfriend Jason. They were waiting for the rain to stop or at least reduce to a light sprinkle so she could get out without getting soaked. She hated the fact that she was stuck playing the good girl with her parents, always tryng to act so innocent and clueless, simply because anything else would mean losing access to her trust. She had till she turned 25 before she could get rid of the act. *They'd be shocked when they find out that I'm not such a good girl*, she thought snidely.

She glanced at Jason and he grinned at her.

"You look beautiful," he whispered and stroke her thigh, letting his fingers stray higher.

She giggled. "You've been saying that the whole night."

"Because you do. Shit, you looking fine as hell tonight," answered Jason.

"Only tonight?"

"You know what I mean," Jason said grinning and moving in closer to Kimberly

She laughed again. "Thank you."

Kimberly was still surprised that she fell for him. Initially, she only started hanging out with him to make her parents upset. She just knew they would hate him for her. Jason was a known street kid whose stepfather was infamous for being one of the biggest drug dealers in Oakland back in the early 90s. Story has it that his stepfather, who was much more of a father to him was killed during a drug deal that went wrong. Jason never liked talking about him and she always wondered why. Her parents on, the other hand, felt Jason was headed down the same path as his stepfather and wanted her as far away from him as possible.

"Thanks for the puppy," she said.

He shrugged. "Anything for you, shorty," he said before leaning in to kiss her.

His lips were soft and tasted like mint and marshmallows, she almost chuckled at the weird combination. Slowly, he lifted her top up with his hands and brushed over her covered breasts. She moaned as he moved his other hand and slid them inside her pants, his fingers getting closer till he touched her clit and she moaned again. Jason removed his hands and untangled their lips, then he removed his shirt and looked at her.

"Come on, take your clothes off," he said, out of breath.

She giggled awkwardly. "Er, Jason. I don't think we should do that," she told him. She wasn't going to let her first time be in a car and just a few steps away from her parents' house.

"Not this again," Jason groaned and looked away.

Kimberly touched his face but he shrugged her hand off. "I want you to understand that this isn't something I want to do on a whim."

He shot a sharp gaze at her. "A whim? I've been trying for months, and it's fucking frustrating." He paused and looked away again, trying not to raise his voice. "Almost feels as if I'm forcing myself on you or something. Tons of girls out there, you know. Why would you push me to them?"

She bit her lip and closed her eyes. She couldn't lose him to those skanks who'd open their legs for anyone. *No way.*

Jason stopped unzipping his Levi's but she sighed and reached over to finish unzipping the pants for him.

"But I can do this," she whispered in his ear as she clasped his hardness in her hand. She heard him gasp, then tried to push her hand away.

"No, stop. I am..." he started to say but his voice was muffled by a gasp when she began moving her hands up and down his shaft, all the while whispering dirty talks in his ear. She could tell it turned him on as he was moaning and groaning with pleasure.

"Damn," Jason breathed. "Your hand feels so good."

Kimberly reached in front of her seat to grab her purse, she pulled out her travel sized hand cream and squeezed a small amount into her hand, and rubbed it on his hardness, making it smooth and easier to glide on. She moved slowly. Too slowly, hands clasped a little tighter and fingers brushing the tip of his dick.

"Faster," he said-almost shouting.

"Not yet darling, not yet."

Still moving with torturous slowness, she worked him, up and down, up and down. Jason was soon muttering gibberish, his lips parted. Until he was arching his hips and grinding against the palm of her hands, trying to force faster movement. He was practically sobbing from desperation.

"So good. I'm so close," he groaned. "Put it in your mouth."

She continued stroking, pretending not to hear him. Jason grabbed her head and tried to pull her mouth to his dick. "Jas-" she muttered and pushed against his efforts.

He groaned and clicked his tongue.

"I guess you're also waiting for the right time to give a nigga some head," he said flatly. She hesitated, still clasping the dick throbbing in her hand. After a few moments, she placed her knees on the seat and bent over, taking his dick into her mouth.

Jason threw his head back and smiled. "Finally! That's it, fuck!"

Her lips smacked and she moaned while sucking his dick, moving her head up and down and not even using her teeth. *Damn, sure this is your first time?* He wanted to ask, but he was so much on cloud nine to bother.

"Tell me when you're about to... you know," she reminded him, looking up.

"Yeah, yeah, whatever," he grunted and pushed her head back down. He kept his hand firm on her head, pumping his dick in and out of her mouth, while she struggled to keep up. Kimberly tried to push back when his dick suddenly throbbed, and she felt his cum spurting inside her mouth.

She fell back, eyebrows bent, looking pissed as she wiped her mouth.

He was so out of breath, all she could hear was his loud panting.

She reached for her purse and grabbed a wipe out of it. She glared at him. "I told you to let me know..."

"Oh, come on, babe," Jason chuckled. He was all smiles, obviously delighted by the blowjob. She couldn't stay mad at him, not when he was looking at her that way and also stroking her hair tenderly.

"Feel better now big baby?" She asked, with a hint of attitude.

He pulled her close. "I couldn't control myself, it felt so good... you were too good. I just lost my sense."

That made her smile. Kimberly likes Jason and knows he wouldn't wait much longer to have sex with her, he would get it from someone else. She wiped him off and gave him a kiss, then reached for the dog in the backseat and picked it up.

"Thanks. Goodnight," she said, stepping out the car just as it started to sprinkle again.

Kimberly groaned and ran down to her house. Carefully, she snuck in the huge gates, trying her best to make sure her parents didn't hear her or her new puppy, in case it decided to bark. She tiptoed to the front door and pressed her finger onto the digital scan keypad right beside the knob. It scanned her and she quickly slide in.

Her cell phone buzzed as soon as she got in, and her heart skipped a beat. She relaxed when she saw it was Thea, she declined the call and responded with a text telling her that she would call her back.

A loud thud startled her and she jumped. Kimberly froze for a moment thinking the noise was coming from the storage shed but soon noticed her dad had forgotten to put the lock back on... again. The door was swinging against the wind, but she was reluctant to walk over to the shed to secure it. Not in the dark, anyway. *I'll just let dad know in the morning.*

She walked the few feet to the living room. Her father, still dressed in what he called his stepping-out clothes. Kimberly figured he and her mom must have had a date night and he drank too much to make it up the stairs. She'd seen it before. He was out on the couch with his 90's R&B playlist still going. *Typical!*

Kimberly tiptoed past him to the kitchen and opened the counter cabinet to grab a water bowl for the dog, then walked to the sink to fill it up. She was turning off the tap when she saw a dark human-shaped figure standing in the middle of their backyard directly facing the kitchen window, but it was only there for a second, so she convinced herself it was nothing; her mind must be playing tricks on her. *Besides, the security system would've been triggered if someone was actually out there.* Kimberly walked out of the kitchen and tiptoed past her dad again, headed upstairs past her parents' room to her room. Gently closing the door, she put down the dog and removed her shoes and the hoodie, then she quickly put together a makeshift bed out of her many decorative pillows.

Kimberly picked her new puppy up and gave it the water to drink. "You are just a little ball of cuteness, aren't you?" She asked, adorably rubbing its ears.

She slowly put the dog down on the bed and walked to her closet. After spending some of her nighttime outside, Kimberly couldn't wait to go to bed. But first, she wanted to call Thea back to tell her what just happened with Jason. She quietly went to the bathroom for a warm towel to clean herself with.

Staring at how soaked her panties were, she couldn't believe sucking Jason could do that to her. Yeah, he could be an asshole, she admitted to herself, but she liked it when he was being rough with her. If there had been any doubt before, her soaked panties wiped that away. Kimberly put on her silk pajamas and went to lay on the bed, but as she was drifting off, she heard the dog whimpering and rubbing its body against the bed. She sighed and picked it up. "Okay, then I guess you sleep with

Mommy tonight," she said, placing it next to her on the bed.

She called Thea, excited to tell her what she did with Jason; it would be so thrilling to unload the juicy details. As soon as Thea's voice came up, Kimberly felt the excitement surge.

"I also have something to tell you, but you go first," Thea said when Kim gushed about what she had to say.

"Okay, okay," she giggled and went on to tell her what just happened, but when Thea let out a series of grunts and her responses they were far below what Kim expected. Sensing that something was wrong, she asked, "Do you have a problem with my man?"

Thea's voice got salty when she responded. "Ugh, I saw that nigga at the AMC movie theatre, boo'd up with ho-ass Amara from way back in high school."

Kimberly froze and her lips trembled. *What?* She wanted to say but her words got stuck in her throat. There was no controlling the waterworks. She was about to respond when the alarm went off.

The shrill sound was followed by a loud sound of glass shattering downstairs, followed by scuffling sounds and multiple footsteps. She sat up; eyes wide open with fear. Someone burst into her room, and she wanted to scream but it was her mother.

"Mom, what"

Mrs. Bell rushed towards her, a shotgun in her hand. "I will explain it later. What I need you to do right now sweetie, is to get into your closet and hide. Wait! Is that a puppy? Take it with you. Just hide, okay?" She was sounding way too calm for the commotion going on downstairs.

She hung up on Thea without releasing a word.

Kim has seen her mom shoot guns before at the range. But this was the first time she has seen her in action and planning to shoot at human targets. She looked so ready, so... natural. *This wasn't her first time.* Confused, Kim stood up from the bed, picked up the puppy, and headed for the closet.

Her Mom shoved her slightly. "Go on!" She said.

Before the wooden doors closed, Kimberly heard her dad's grunt from downstairs and then someone yell, "Where is it?"

9

4 HOURS EARLIER

The glasses clinked and Kimbella's eyes lit up.

"I didn't really see you as the romantic type, Steven," she said and sipped her wine, tasting it slowly and licking her lips.

"You're trying to tease me, aren't ya?" Steven asked through a soft smile.

She moved her shoulders playfully and returned the smile. He wanted to focus on their romantic date and make it as lovely as possible, but his eyes would occasionally shift to the front door of the restaurant.

It was a lovely evening and Kimbella remarked on it. Keeping himself in the moment, he gazed at her and nodded in agreement.

"It was almost like this when we first met," he said and Kim's eyes sparkled as a soft squeal escaped her lips, her mind tugged back to that moment.

Steven reached forward and took her hand. "And if I remember correctly, it felt just as magical as tonight because I met you."

She blushed and giggled, smacked his shoulder and lightly grazing his arm with her fingernails.

"You're teasing me."

He leaned closer, his eyes shifting to the front door for a short moment, and whispered, "No, I'm not."

"I guess you were all fired up that night because someone pumped me up full of his nut and I conceived," she laughed softly and squeezed his hand.

"Speaking of our girl," Kimbella added. "Her attitude sure has changed since we told her about the trust and the conditions for getting it."

Steven smiled. "Yeah, she's suddenly someone else, nicer and sweet."

Kimbella laughed. "If we knew this would make her act right, we should have told her sooner."

Steve chuckled at that. He was about to make a comment when the front door opened. His eyes became sharp, his focus shifting away from Kimbella's voice.

"Uh-huh," he let out a distracted response, not sure what Kimbella said. She frowned and let go of his hand.

"Steven, what's going on?" She asked.

He said nothing, still watching the traffic of people entering and exiting the restaurant. He would have loved to enjoy the general aesthetic of the place the smooth lights and nice music but other things occupied his mind.

Kimbella's voice cut sharply through his reverie and

he glanced at her. He saw the mix of worry and annoyance plastered on her face.

"What's going on?"

He sighed, his face sagged with lines of worry spreading over it.

"It's nothing," he answered.

But it didn't feel like nothing. Kimbella wanted to ask again when a man walked into the restaurant. He stood at the front door, hands in his coat pockets, and glanced in Steve's direction. Something about the suspicious way he looked at her man made her curious.

He was rough around the edges, that man; a dark contrast to the vibrant atmosphere of the restaurant. He looked like he'd missed his way and stepped into the restaurant by mistake, certainly not like someone out to enjoy himself.

Kimbella observed him once more before looking back at Steven. When the man took a seat at a table and was soon occupied by the menu, Steven relaxed a bit.

He met Kim's accusatory stare and chuckled.

"Your eyes say a lot, you know that?"

She pouted and narrowed her eyes, her way of telling him to explain himself.

"Okay, maybe there's something."

She rolled her eyes and gestured for him to continue.

Taking another deep breath and fighting the urge to take another glance at the sketchy guy, Steven opened up.

"The FBI came to my office today..."

"The FBI?" Kimbella asked in a hushed voice, arching her eyebrows. "What did they want?"

"They came with a bunch of questions about my connection with Phil. They were using terms like 'trafficking' and 'cartel mules'." He paused and took in the expression on Kim's face. She listened intently; her eyes set. Steven always admired her strength and resolve, and that showed right now in how she processed what he laid out without entering into panic mode.

"That's much deeper than the initial agreement we had with Phil," he continued and she nodded. It was supposed to be only intel on wiretaps, confidential informants, and possible drug raids, not human and cross-border drug trafficking; that was a whole new level.

"The feds are getting close," Steven said flexing his jaw, taking a deep breath. "I'm not willing to risk the lives of my family for anything."

Another pause and he let his eyes fall on his untouched drink. A waiter walked past and he ordered a glass of water.

"Need anything?" The waiter asked Kimbella and she shook her head slowly, her mind already preoccupied.

Steven gulped down the water after it came, sighing softly. A quick glance at the sketchy man still focused on his meal, it seemed. He faced Kimbella again.

"What's the plan?"

He stared at the empty glass of water, following a lone drop of water sliding down the smooth surface and getting lost in the depths of the glass.

"It's either I work with the feds in witness protection," his words halted slightly as his mind conjured these images in his head. "Or we run away, out of the country before shit really hits the fan."

The options hung heavily in the air, followed by a lingering silence only disturbed by the low chatter around them, and the clinking of cutleries on plates.

"Well, we aren't snitching to the feds," Kimbella finally spoke, her voice controlled. She was the daughter of a once high-powered street hustler, so she understood what that meant. There was no way she'd dabble into snitch culture, no matter what.

Before Steven could respond, another man walked in. He caught the movement through the corner of his eyes and glanced in that direction. The man was just as disheveled and out of place as the other one. There were similarities, he just couldn't put his finger on it. The hostess already spotted him and had directed her path toward him. Steven knew she'd direct him to sit with the other guy, and that might double his worry, but they did the opposite. She walked him across the room and sat at another table.

Neither of the odd-looking men acknowledged the other or showed any signs that they knew one another. Just a random coincidence that two odd fellas would walk into the same restaurant, but the idea didn't sit well with Steven.

A sudden movement at his side caused his heart to thump, and the hairs on his arms raised.

"It's just the waiter," Kimbella whispered, now looking more worried than before.

"Your food will be right out," the waiter said, after bringing out some bread.

"Sounds good," he mumbled.

A minute later Kimbella glanced at him. "I'm gonna use the restroom real quick."

She pushed her chair back and stood up, and like the perfect gentleman, Steven also stood up as she excused herself from the table.

"You're sweet," she whispered and touched his arm.

Steven turned around and noticed odd-guy number one and two, both turned away from looking in their direction. He kept his eyes on them but they kept their eyes on their respective tables, putting up the flimsy images of people focused on their dining experience.

Steven sat back down and stroke his chin, *something's up with those two.*

Rubbing his hands together, frowning when he noticed how sweaty they were–he took deep breaths.

Just relax, Steven, you're just being paranoid. He sipped his wine and wished those guys hadn't shown up. He wished the freaking feds hadn't shown up at his office, and that this could have just been a normal romantic evening.

The wine was tasteless in his mind, and he quickly realized his thumping heart and edgy nerves wouldn't let him rest. Steven's chair screeched when he got up and headed in the direction of the bathroom. Odd-guy number two glanced at him.

Steven passed the waiter taking the food to their table and caught up with Kimbella coming out the bathroom.

Her eyes widened when she saw him. "I wasn't gone *that* long, was I?"

His response was to grab her arm. "We're leaving."

She didn't argue as he led her through the kitchen and out the back of the restaurant.

"What is going on?" She finally asked, when he let go of her arm.

"Something feels off in that restaurant," he replied and rubbed his head, his eyes darting around. "I didn't feel... safe.

She took his hand and squeezed tenderly, offering her warm smile. "I think the visit from the feds got you wrapped up tight. You need to relax, okay?

"Yeah, that's true," he agreed, but deep down he suspected it might be more than just paranoia. There was no use dwelling on it for now, he told himself.

"I'm going to make up for tonight, I promise," Steven said and pulled her close for a kiss.

Her eyes shone and she laughed. "You better."

The front door clicked shut and low beeps came up when Kimbella entered the security code to the alarm system. The stiffness eased out a little now that they had entered the house. Steven headed straight to the den and dropped himself on the couch, stretching out and exhaling deeply. His eyes were closed while he consciously tried to push back whatever fears were creeping inside his mind.

Kimbella's voice echoed through the house.

"Kimberly!" She called out to their daughter several times without getting any response.

The couch groaned when Steven turned and opened his eyes.

"Where has that girl gone to this time?" Kimbella said, standing by the door.

"I think she said something about going out with her friends. She's probably not back yet."

Her lips stretched into a sexy smile, and her eyes sparkled.

"I know that look," Steven said with a short laugh.

"We have the house all to ourselves," she said and walked over to him. She climbed on top of him and gently massaged his chest. "You know what that means, right?"

Of course, he did. But he wasn't in the mood right now, he wanted to tell her. The thought of the feds and those sketchy guys were the last things anyone needed on their mind when they had a sexy woman slowly grinding on them.

Kimbella's fingers moved under his shirt, warm against his skin, caressing gently. Her hand was soon on his belt and then, she had Jason's dick in her hand.

A soft grunt tumbled out of his mouth when she squeezed his shaft and pulled it up and down, letting it harden in her grasp.

"Someone's waking up," Kimbella whispered in *that* sexy voice. She knew it turned him on when she let her voice float smoothly through the air like a soul singer.

Her warm breath wrapped around the tip of his dick

when she parted her lips and pressed down on it slowly, letting him feel every touch. Caressing the base of his dick, she pushed her head down and let the length slide up into her mouth.

A muffled moan escaped her lips when she tightened them around the now-hardened dick inside her mouth.

Steven closed his eyes and forget about all his concerns, enjoying the wet lips on his dick, and the tongue sliding along his shaft. She made slow up-and-down motions with her left hand and let out slurping sounds when she started bobbing her head up and down. "Mmm...yeah."

Kimbella gasped when he thrust his dick up against the back of her throat.

His breath quickened after a while, and he pushed her head down, thrusting his dick faster into her mouth until he shoved it up one last time, letting out a long groan, and came inside her mouth. Kimbella moaned and sucked hard on his shaft, gulping down the thick, hot fluid shooting down her throat. He let go and she pulled up slowly, sliding her tongue over the veiny dick.

She would have grabbed his dick and stroked it until he became hard again, then straddle him and ride him all night, but he was tired.

"Get some rest now, baby," she whispered and kissed him. Steven moved his hand to her ass and gave it a light squeeze.

"Don't tempt me," she giggled.

Steven soon drifted off to sleep on the couch, snoring

lightly, Kimbella got up to go take a shower. Stopping at Kimberly's room first, she peeked in. Sometimes her daughter would fall asleep with her headphones on—she had cautioned her about that so many times but her room was empty, so she continued to the master bedroom to shower.

10

PRESENT

Kimbella was perplexed to see a puppy and made a mental note to ask Kimberly about it later.

She glanced down at her daughter. "You have got to be extremely quiet and call the police. I'll be back," she told her.

Kim whimpered. "Mom, what is going on downstairs? Is someone trying to rob us?"

"I said I will explain everything later. Just do what I say, and you will be fine."

She was terrified but chose to trust her mom. Reluctantly, Kimberly nodded but with so many questions floating around in her mind. "Can't you stay and wait for the cops with me?" She asked, trembling.

"No, honey. I have to go help your father," said her mother.

Kimbella quickly closed the door and rushed out of the room. The house was eerily silent. She slowly started descending the stairs, her heart pounding fast. When she reached the end of the staircase and gasped loudly when she saw a trail of blood. She clasped her mouth shut with her hands, tears falling down her cheeks. Kimbella followed the trail which led her to the garage door where she stopped abruptly and turned around, scared and confused when someone grabbed her by the throat. She kicked and flayed her hands blindly. Kimbella's gun was knocked out of her hand and the assailant lifted her off her feet by the throat, she wheezed and gasped for air, slamming her fist into the assailant's shoulder blade.

"Ahgh!" The man grunted and tightened his grip on her throat.

Kimbella struggled longing for unrestricted air and kicked the person, but it was of no use, she couldn't get free. She clawed at the man's face, dipping her fingernails into his skin and drawing blood. The man focused on squeezing Kimbella's neck, despite the blood scratches on his face.

Kimbella was losing consciousness due to the blockage of air. She felt someone else prick her with a needle and while dazed she felt was being drugged and pushed into the back of a van. The drugs were kicking in fast. First, she felt nauseous, then drowsy, sick, then bewildered, and before she passed out.

Back in her room, Kim was hearing the commotion from inside the closet. She brought out her phone and with shaking hands, dialed 911. The call was picked up at the first ring, but then it was hung up before she was able to say anything. She tried again but got the same results.

Without a second thought, Kimberly opened the closet and stepped out. She thought it would be better if she went outside and got help. Just as she was walking out the bedroom, she heard multiple footsteps running up the stairs. She turned around swiftly and ran back into the room. Kimberly tried to push her dresser in front of the door but it was way too heavy to move. She took deep breaths and tried to steady her trembling hands. She managed to push her bookshelf in front of the door but it wasn't nearly heavy enough to stop the goons from coming in. It was an obstacle for sure but an easy one to get through. She moved away from the door, her mind racing fast. With her eyes darting around the room, she searched for a weapon.

Good enough, Kimberly thought and grabbed her tennis racket. She snuck out the bedroom window the same way she did whenever she was going out to see Jason, except this time she felt more pressure, and her heart thumped against her chest, like she'd suddenly woken up on the ledge of a really tall building. She jumped down and heard a snap in her leg, Kimberly placed her hand on her mouth and yelled into it in agony. She had sprained her ankle in the process making it even harder to escape.

"Oh shit!" She cursed as she held unto the wall for support. Sweating, she limped her way towards the front of the house hoping to get to her neighbors.

The goons, however, tore up the room searching for her, but no avail, she wasn't there. One of them leaned on the wall inside her room and texted a guy waiting outside, 'The girl's not here.'

The person texted back, 'I found her. She's right here, clean up and get out.'

Meanwhile, Kim saw someone a few houses down sitting in a white security vehicle apparently listening to music. She hurried to the car, as fast as her injured leg could go, and knocked on the window all the while glancing back to make sure she was not being followed. The guy rolled down the window and narrowed his eyes at her. "Hey, what's wrong?" He asked with a hint of worry.

Kimberly tried to catch her breath. "Some... thu... thugs in my house. My momma and daddy... they are in there!" She said, frantically trying to catch her breath.

"Whoa, slow down. Are you saying there are dangerous people in the house with your parents?" The man asked.

Kim nodded her head anxiously. "I tried calling the police but my phone wouldn't connect."

His brows twitched perplexedly and he quickly brought out his phone. He turned it on and as Kim watched, he dialed a number. He put the phone to his ear. Kim kept turning her head back and forth.

"Weird," she heard the man say, bringing her attention back to him. "Mine isn't going through either."

"Oh, my God!" She almost wailed.

The light rain turned to a pour.

"Why don't you get in and I can drive you to the station and get help? Is that okay with you?"

Kim sighed in relief, "Yes. Yes, it is." She opened the door to the car and carefully got in. "Thanks," she said, attempting to put on seatbelts.

Suddenly, the guy elbowed her head against the window and put a knife to her throat. Blood oozed from her head and the knife he had against her throat was penetrating her neck splitting it open.

She gargled and attempted to push the knife away. "Please?!" Kim beseeched, choking. "Take the knife off my throat!"

"Shut the fuck up, bitch!" He shouted.

He then brought out his phone and dialed a number. "I got the little bitch, she's in the van with me. Meet me outside. Hurry up," he said to the person on the other side.

Kimberly noticed her puppy in a neighbor's yard when the van stopped to pick up the three guys exiting her home, running across the driveway while another white van pulled out after them. One of them, a heavily built guy opened the door and threw a black pillowcase over her head, and zip-tied her hands. Kimberly was then yanked to the backseat and laid across them in an attempt to conceal her. She felt someone trying to grope her, causing her to clench her jaws in disgust.

"The hell, man? Stop touching all over her you fucking perv!" She heard someone else say and breathed a sigh of relief.

The first guy grunted disrespectfully. "Yeah? What are you gonna do about it?"

"Let's not make it bigger than what it needs to be,

man. We had a job to do and that's it. You know it's not right for you to put your hands on practically every female you encounter. Does that shit ever land you some pussy?"

"Consensual pussy that is?" The other guy said shaking his head.

"You know what, I am about done with your bullshit, Asher. Why don't you mind your own fucking business, what are you a faggot or some shit?"

"Stop it, both of you," said a familiar voice from the front seat.

The driver, Kimberly believe clearly, he was the man in charge because both shut the fuck up and the pig stopped groping her. "Put her to sleep," he said.

A plastic crackling sound ensued, then seconds later she felt a sharp ache in her arm. Kimberly felt her eyes getting heavy before she drifted off into a slumber she won't remember having.

11

The sound of something dripping woke Kimberly up with a pulsating headache. She sat up shivering from the coldness. She touched her face and found the pillowcase was still over her head. She struggled to take it off but couldn't. Kimberly sighed exasperatedly and dropped her hands to the floor. She kept touching the cold concrete ground with her palm, trying to get a feel of where she was. It felt damp and smelt moldy.

"Hello!" She shouted. The echo of her voice suggests she was in a large space. "Where am I?" She asked. Quiet. "What happened to my parents?" She asked again. Still, no one answered. She moved forward with her body. "Listen, whatever it is you want, just tell my parents. Either one of them. They'll give you whatever you want to get me out of here. Just... please let me go!" She pleaded for a deal.

Kimberly heard someone's laughter far away and the shuffling sounds of footsteps approaching her. She figured she must've been alone all this while. Suddenly, the pillowcase was snatched off her head and her eyes welcomed a blinding bright light. Kimberly screeched at the pain from patches of her hair being ripped off along with the pillowcase. She squinted her eyes and tried to take in where she was. A huge round space with low ceilings as low as the hobbit's dwelling. From the dim light coming in from what appeared to be a basement window, the place looked murky. Looked like Tyrion's dungeon in *Game of Thrones*.

Spider webs and junk decorated it like a slummy garage sale just waiting to happen.

Kimberly adjusted her eyes to look at the people standing in front of her. There were three of them, two were white and tall and the other one was black like her and much shorter. They were all looking down at her with unreadable expressions on their faces. Kimberly shivered with fear.

Since this was a kidnapping, her abductors were letting her see them. They don't care about Kimberly telling because she'll end up dead. She screamed internally, the most gruesome episode of *Criminal Minds* running through her mind with flashy images in a space of a heartbeat.

"Quit making so much damn noise, will you? We could hear you all the way upstairs. Your parents are now angels, they are both gone," said the black guy. Just then, Kimberly realized he was the one who drove the car, the one who offered to help her. Chills ran down her spine and her throat dried up. Kimberly's folks weren't exactly 'parents of the year', and they weren't really close ever since sending her away to live with her grandmother when she was only eight. Kimberly felt a wave of sadness at the news of their deaths. *No one deserved to be killed just like that and for what reason,* she thought. What would it have been like if she had bonded more with her parents? Would she be where she was now? The guilt was heavy, and creeping with sadness.

He crouched down in front of her. "We're only keeping you alive because we were paid extra in a side deal, you'll be worth much more to a friend of ours in Israel," he said, looking totally pleased with himself. "We're not done here until we're paid the rest of our money for getting rid of your parents. Once that is done, we'll get out of the country and sell you to a loaded buyer in Israel. Hope you can speak Spanish, la puta," he winked.

By now, Kim's heart was pounding fast and her brain went numb from fear. She whimpered, "No! No! Please just let me go, okay? I have lots of money. I... I can offer you double of whatever the person who hired you is paying."

The man snickered and shook his head. One of the guys standing smacked her hard and was about to hit her again when the other guy held his hand to stop him.

"Caleb, no," the black guy said. Caleb glared at him before jerking his hand away.

"You shouldn't worry too much, doll. I told you the buyer is filthy rich; you'll be well taken care of... that's if you cooperate. Plus, there will be sex, lots and lots of sex," the other one said sinisterly and Caleb laughed hard.

"No! Someone help me. Please!" Kimberly shouted, utterly freaked out.

The man stood up and smiled at her. "You can scream all you want, but no one will hear you. No one's coming for you. And by the way, since we'll be spending quite some time together, you should know our names," he said. "I am Elijah, this is Caleb and that is Asher," he added before turning around to leave. "Don't touch her, Caleb," he warned.

She figured he must be the one who wanted to grope her earlier in the car and quickly looked at him, frightened. He gave her a wicked grin and raised his eyebrows. Caleb was known for raping women back in Boston and their native home Tel Aviv, Israel.

The two keep her locked in the windowless room. They fed her and allowed her to shower, but only if it was done in front of them. Kimberly would object, but Caleb only shouted at her. He was enjoying every part of it, and she could tell. Asher, however, turned around a bit, and after some time, he walked out of the room and came back shortly after, holding something.

"What's that?" asked Caleb.

"Clothes. Figured she should change," Asher answered, handing them to her.

"And since when did you start figuring out what people should do?" Caleb asked, annoyed.

Kim collected the clothes. She gave a small smile, "Thank you."

Two days later

Asher and Caleb were upstairs watching the television, and Kim was still locked away in the room. Asher's phone rang and he picked it up, it was Elijah calling about an urgent situation. He ended the call and looked at Caleb. "That was Elijah. I have to leave. Watch the girl," he said and rushed out.

Caleb smirked. This is the moment he had been waiting for, to be alone with Kim. He couldn't wait to go downstairs and force himself onto her.

Kimberly had just woken from a nap when Caleb opened the door and came in to stand in front of her, all 6'5 and 45% muscle of him. He didn't even bother to close the door.

She slowly sat up from the mattress, feeling a bit weary. "Uh, hey," she said.

Caleb smiled and approached her. He stoops down and grinned widely. "What do you say before we send you off, I give you the sex of a lifetime? Personally, I enjoy taking what I want from women. So feel free to fight me," he said and laughed like a maniac. He traced a finger on her face and then sniffed in her hair.

"Mmm, so good," he said.

Kim moved further away and he followed her. He removed his shirt and tried to remove her clothes. She punched him in the groin and he looked up at her, infuriated. Caleb tossed her around the room, knocking down and breaking a wooden picture frame from the wall. He then began to forcefully tear off her clothes.

"Stop trying to fight this, you know it's what you want," he leered, sticking out his tongue and running it along the side of her neck. "'You little cock-tease." His fingers moved over her body, creeping along her skin and causing goosebumps to arise.

Kimberly cried out and tried to fight him off. In the process, her hands touched a piece of glass from the broken frame. Caleb was moaning into her neck and licking on her ear lobe. Disgusted, she rammed the glass into the side of *his* neck. Caleb fell heavily on her body causing her to struggle to get him off, Kimberly got up and ran out of the room and up the stairs making sure she locked the door from the outside.

Kimberly panted and glanced around her, not sure if the house was empty. Her heart beat painfully fast and her lips trembled. Spotting the front door, she dashed towards it.

The front door was also open, she pushed it and got out of the house. Having no idea where she was going, she started running into the woods.

Her legs were bruised and bleeding. Her bare feet snapped on broken branches, and her toes clipped painfully against stones. She fought through the pain, running through the woods and grunting each time her skin got grazed by a rugged branch, or her legs scratched by sharp grass. Kimberly panted and surged forward, her body pumping enough adrenaline to fight through the pain.

"Ahh!" She squealed when she tripped over a branch and fell on the ground, rolling through the dirt. She picked herself up and continued.

She must have run for almost half an hour before she saw a rundown parking lot of a motel. Kimberly rushed inside, but there was no one by the counter. She started banging at a random room door, and a middle-aged woman opened the door.

"Please. You have to help me. I..." she started saying, but the woman slammed the door in her face.

Kimberly rushed to the next room, and then the next, but more than half of them ignored her, and the few that answered all gave the same reaction. She exhaustingly reached Room 109 and knocked; she wasn't going to give up. Surprisingly, the door opened and a man stood there. He looked almost excited at first, but his face dropped when he saw her face.

"Oh," he said.

12

The guy who opened the door stepped back and stared down at her with scanning brown eyes, long curly hair falling down his back shoulder length. She gathered he must be in his mid-twenties.

"Who you? What do you want?" He asked, looking disappointed.

Without answering, Kimberly walked past him into the room, expecting to see a lady. He followed her inside, leaving the door open. "Hey, what the hell do you think you're doing? Get" he started to say.

"Are you here alone?" She interrupted him.

"Er, yeah," he answered, astonished. She nodded and went to close the door, then she went to peek out the window, hoping no one was after her.

"You mind telling me what the hell you want and who the fuck are you?" she heard him ask. "Look, whatever it is you got mixed up in, I don't want no parts of it. So please..." he gestured towards the door. "Get out!"

She pushed back and held his wrist, begging him to understand. He broke free and grunted indifferently, "I got my own problems."

Kimberly turned around and rushed towards him. "Listen, you gotta help me. I was taken and my parents… my parents," she whimpered. "Just help me! Call the police, okay? Please."

He folded his arms, looking baffled. "Sorry, but I can't do that shorty."

"What? Why? I just told you I was kidnapped. I was assaulted, I barely got away. It's just a matter of time before they find me," said a frightened Kim.

He sighed. "Look, I'm sorry for all the troubles you went through, but I can't help you. I can't call the cops. There's a store right across the street, go there, I'm sure you will find someone with a phone."

Her jaw dropped with shock. Kimberly looked around the room for a phone until she found one, then made her way towards it. Loon hurried after her, he grabbed the phone away from the wall before she could touch it. "Whoa! What do you think you are doing?" He asked.

"I'm calling the police," she said.

"You don't understand. You can't call the police," he lowered his voice. "I will get arrested. I'm on the run from the feds."

Kim furrowed her brows in astonishment, she wasn't sure why but felt safe, like she could trust the man. Plus, something about him reminded her of Jason.

"Can I call my boyfriend then?" She asked.

"No," he shook his head. "Calling anyone at all will draw attention to me. You can go away in the distance and call whoever you want to."

Kimberly ran across the bed and knocked off the pillows. Stopping short, her eyes fell on the gun underneath the pillow. Loon also stopped and eyed the gun. For a second, they eyed the gun and each other, then they both jumped for it.

Her hand fell on the gun first and she pulled it back and leveled it at him.

"Just let me explain," she panted.

He raised both hands and approached her slowly. "Drop the gun."

Her hands trembled and she moved a few steps back. "Just listen to me!"

"Please, put down the gun," he pleaded.

Kimberly rolled her eyes, let out an exasperated grunt, and turned the gun on her chin.

"Whoah! Don't even think about it... I'm in enough trouble already!" He shouted.

"I can't leave," she blurted out. "By now, I'm sure they are aware that I'm missing. Can I just stay here for today?"

There was a long pause of silence as he contemplated her request. Then to his own surprise, he said, "Sure." Still skeptical of the situation. Loon couldn't risk her being traced to him anyway.

"Oh, thank you. Can I use your bathroom? I need to

change, I feel disgusting," she said with a grimace. She could literally smell the awful stench Caleb left on her.

He pointed his hand in the direction of a bathroom door and she followed it, muttering thanks. She stopped halfway and glanced back. "I forgot to introduce myself. I am Kimberly Bell. My, er, friends just call me Kim. You are...?"

He pursed his lips and nodded. "Johnson. Loon Johnson."

She smiled. "Nice to meet you, Loon."

"Likewise."

Kim noticed the bottles of lotions and scrubs and feminine products. She spotted an open suitcase with women's clothes in it. *I thought he said he was alone,* she wondered.

Her curiosity got the best of her, so she stepped out and asked him about it.

"It's uh, well it belongs to..." he stopped, unsure of how to explain it. She noticed he was getting visibly upset the more he tried to explain.

"I'll explain later," he sighed.

She agreed but thought it was a bit strange.

"I'll go have that shower now," she said and he nodded without looking at her.

As Kimberly turned on the shower and the warm water began to wash away all the dirt and residue on her body, her heart was heaving. She tried to take multiple deep breaths, in order to calm herself down but ended up breaking down. She placed her hands on her mouth and cried her heart out thinking about all she had been through and survived in the past few days.

Her parents being murdered, the kidnapping, the assault, damn near getting raped, and possibly murdering a man. Kim stared at the wounds and bruises on her body. How has her life come to this?

When she came out of the bathroom, Kim saw a dress on the bed and takeout food on the table. She guessed Loon must have laid it out for her. The dress was a little too wide for her at the hip, but she wouldn't be picky. She was tying her hair up when Loon came into the room.

"Hey," she said. "Thanks for the food and clothes."

"You're welcome," he said and went to sit on the bed. "So here's the thing, I'm going to leave early morning tomorrow. You can use the room for a bit longer if you want, I'll pay."

She nodded, sitting on the chair. "Grateful," she said. "So, are you like a businessman or something? Got in a bit of a problem, people looking for you and you tryna escape?"

Loon raised his eyebrows at her, no doubt surprised that she is directly asking him a personal question after barely meeting him an hour ago.

She chuckled apologetically. "Sorry, if I'm being nosy."

Loon nodded and stood up. "You can take the bed if you want, I'll sleep on the floor," he said.

In less than half an hour, Loon fell asleep with his gun under his pillow. Kim wondered why he went to sleep so early and figured it must be because he wanted to hit the roads early morning.

Loon woke up and noticed Kim wasn't in the room with him. He jumped up, alarmed, and went to the bathroom to check on her, but she wasn't there. He rushed out to the parking lot and walked around the motel but still, there was no sign of her. He felt bad and wondered if she had ran away, but he went into the bathroom again to wash his hands, he found her asleep in the bathtub fully clothed.

He sighed with relief and pat her gently on her shoulder, which made her wake up startled with wide eyes.

"Hey, hey. It's me," he said. "It's just me."

Her shoulder fell and she looked down. "Oh, God! I can't believe I fell asleep here."

"Yea me either, shorty."

She sighed and used her hand to ruffle her hair. She looked up at him, with moist chocolate eyes and in that moment, Loon realized how beautiful she was. A chunk of her hair was down her face, almost completely covering up her left eye.

Suddenly, they heard a heavy knock at the door. Loon's heart skips a beat. He turned to her. "No matter what happens, no matter what you hear, stay here. Do you understand me?"

She nodded frantically. "Yes."

He immediately stood up and exited the bathroom,

Loon snatched up his gun from under the pillow and went to see who it was.

Opening the door, he saw two men, a white and a black man standing there.

He cursed internally, hoping this wasn't some kind of a second warning from Meir. The guys looked like thugs. Not minding hiding his gun, Loon glared at them. "What do ya'll want?"

The short one smiled and stretched his hands out. "Hi. My name is Elijah, and I'm so sorry for troubling you. But we're looking for a young lady who ran away from our care. Traces led us to this building, so we're here asking room by room."

"I haven't seen anybody around here," Loon said, refusing to shake his hand.

"Look, you don't understand. This situation here is critical. She's my friend's daughter and this is not her first time running away from home," said Elijah, face laced with worry.

Loon just pursed his lips and stared.

"She rambles about crazy things like kidnappings and killings. Bizarre stuff like that," Elijah went on. "We need to find her as soon as possible and get her back on her meds. The last time something like this happened, she got hurt."

Loon nodded slowly. "Nope. Haven't seen her."

Elijah's smile dropped. "You wouldn't mind if we come in and check then?" He asked, trying to push his way into the room.

Loon used his body to block the room. "The hell, man?" He said, annoyed.

"We're checking the room," the other guy said, giving Loon a look.

"The hell you are," Loon said, glaring at them.

Elijah pushed at Loon's chest. "Look, man. Why don't we spare each other the theatrics? It's just a search, shouldn't take more than two minutes."

"Yeah? Well, this is my room. I paid for it, and I said..." Loon inclined forward and gritted his teeth. "No," he said, ominously.

Elijah looked like he was going to try harder but instead, he just smiled. "Okay. You're right, it's your room. Fine, but I would like to advise you, sir. This girl is dangerous, she's an addict, and quite frankly not in the right head space. It's extremely critical that we find her."

Loon was getting impatient. "Then go find your girl. Why you still in my face?"

Elijah smiled. "You're right. We'll go," he brought a card out of his pocket. "If you see anything, call me. And refrain from using that gun, I'm very sure you don't have a permit for."

Loon collected the card and slammed the door closed in their faces. He rushed back to the bathroom and found Kim, shivering, her hand holding a knife to her neck.

"What the hell are you doing?" He asked, stunned.

"I heard them. They were here for me, weren't they?

Well, I'd rather die than allow myself to be taken by them again, to go through what I did, again," she sobbed.

Loon tucked his gun in his waistline and moved towards her. "Hey, it's okay. They left. They're gone, alright? Drop the knife, girl. Where did you even find it?"

She cleared her throat. "With your things," she answered, handing the knife over to him.

He nodded. "Come on," he said. They left out of the bathroom and Loon grabbed his duffel bag, then pulled out stacks of money and gave it to her.

"Here. Get yourself somewhere safe."

Kim seemed reluctant. "Do you really have to leave?"

Loon simply shrugged. "Yeah. I have to find the rest of this money in order to pay the maniac that as we speak now, holds my fiancée hostage."

Kim thought for a while before she smirked and looked at him. "How much do you need?"

"4 M's," he said, casually.

She nodded. "What if I can help you get around 2 million at least or more, in exchange for your help to expose the people that murdered my parents? They got... had money."

His eyes widened. "2... 2 million?"

She nodded. "Yup." Seeing the crazy look Loon was giving her, she added, "Once, I found a currency strap in the trash with 10,000 straps around it. Another time I walked into my parents' room when my dad still had the safe open and saw around 100 stacks of money *and* solid gold bars. That was probably a couple million at that time. Point is, they got money. My dad owned the towing company Bella's."

Loon's eyes quivered a little. "Wow," he said, almost inadvertently sarcastic.

"So can we go to my house?"

"Sure. Long as it doesn't involve the police."

Early the next morning, they set out for Kim's house, hoping the killers hadn't already found the hidden safe in her parent's bedroom. They entered the quiet house and Kim stood at the door, transfixed.

"Hey, what is it?" Loon asked.

"Nostalgia," she said, cleaning her tears with the back of her hand. "Follow me."

They passed the lounge and climbed the stairs, and to her surprise, pretty much everything in the house was intact. The wall, the furniture, even the ceramic vases. They reached the bedroom and Kim found the safe, which was still filled with money and expensive jewelry. This was no case of theft or burglary, the goons came for exactly what they wanted, or at least who they wanted her parents.

Blood, broken shards of glass, huge holes in the wall, and knocked over furniture were still everywhere. Loon thought it was strange because there was no evidence of police visiting the scene. Usually, you see police tape, residue from fingerprint gathering, and items marked up for photos. But here there was nothing. He kept his thoughts to himself because he didn't want to scare or worry Kim any more than she already is.

Kim brought out everything from the safe and gave them to Loon. "Here. That's $1,000,000. I thought there was more. I thought the stacks had $10 bands each."

Loon shrugged. "Sometimes money may look like a lot until you count it."

Kim bit her lip. "I know there's more, I just have to get in touch with Phil." Noticing the confused look on Loon's face, she added. "He is my parents' accountant and daddy's right hand man, he is like an Uncle to me," she said, refusing to add that he's also a naughty flirt, always making remarks to her, even when she was underage.

"Alright. How do we talk to him?"

She shrugged. "We would need to drive to his office. It's just downtown on Harrison St."

They stealthily left the house, making sure no one saw them as they got into the car.

"Actually, I am quite puzzled that he hasn't found out about momma and daddy yet... or me yet," said Kim.

They arrived at Phil's office and Kim went in, leaving Loon behind in the car. He was trying to turn on the radio when he saw two familiar guys walking out of the building. He dropped his head, remembering where he saw them. The two guys from the motel, the ones going after Kim. Elijah stopped right across from Loon's car to take a smoke.

"Shit!" He cursed and bent down to hide. The two guys seemed to be in a deep conversation, so he rolled down the window to catch a bit of what they were talking about.

"This old man better give us the rest of our mutha-fuckin' money or we'll be forced to take matters into our own hands. I mean, after the stunt we pulled, he's gonna have his hands full." Elijah was the one talking.

"But what if Phil finds out we no longer have the girl?" Asher asked, obviously worried.

"He won't unless someone tells him," said Elijah, narrowing his eyes at Asher.

Asher shifted uncomfortably. "Yeah, sure."

Elijah nodded and patted him on the back, and the two boys walked off to their separate cars.

Realization hit Loon. They were talking about the same Phil that Kim had gone in to see. Kim was walking into a trap and he has to warn her.

"Oh fuck!" He cursed again. He jumped out of the car and bolted towards the building.

Meanwhile, when Kim entered, the receptionist called Phil to let him know she was in the lobby.

"He'll be down in a few," she said, smiling.

Kim nodded and thanked her, she was relieved. felt this was the safest place for her to be right now. After barely a minute, Philly came out looking utterly surprised to see her, but he quickly hid it with a smile. "Kim... hey," he greeted.

"Phil," she said, standing up to hug him.

"It's nice to see you. Come on, let's go to my office," offered Phil.

While there, Kim told him everything about how her

parents were murdered and how she was kidnapped, assaulted, and almost slaved. Phil's expression went back and forth between shock and disappointment throughout the story.

"God! Kim, I'm so sorry. This must be so hard on you," he said and hugged her again.

She nodded and let go, cleaning her tears.

Phil grinned at her. "But guess what? I know what will cheer you up. Your puppy. It's been at my place this whole time."

Kim looked up at him, baffled. No one knew about the pup, except for Jason and her dearly departed mother. Before she could say anything, Phil stood up. "Sorry, I have to step out for a second. Be right back," he said, gently touching her cheek. The sound of the door locking behind him increased her suspicion.

Philly went into the next office to call Elijah. He was pacing restlessly till the call got answered.

"What the fuck Elijah?!" He yelled.

"Whoa, whoa! Ease up, big guy. What up?"

"Why the fuck? Didn't you tell me you lost Kim? And how did you lose her? Fuck happened?" He asked, truly panicked. "Do you know what you just did? What if she had called the police?"

"H-how did you…?"

"She's in my office right now, you fucking moron. Here's what I want you to do. Get your ass back up here and take her out of here before anyone else sees her, okay? Like right the fuck now! Pronto!"

14

Loon stopped at the directory board, looking for Phil's name. He saw that his office was on the 5th floor, and quickly rushed off, taking the stairs. He thought that would be easier and figured taking the elevator will only draw attention to him. He climbed up, silently praying that nothing had happened to Kim. By the time he reached the floor, his legs were almost numb and he regretted not taking the elevator. He stopped by the receptionist's desk breathing heavily.

"Hi," he said, trying to steady his breathing.

The blonde woman, who must have been in her early 30s looked up. "Hello, sir. How can I help you?"

"I am here to see Philip. It's urgent, where's his office?" Loon asked, trying to play it cool.

The woman's face faltered into a confused look. "Alright, sir. Do you have an appointment?"

"Not really. No," said Loon.

She nodded grimly. "I see. I'm sorry, but he's in a

meeting right now. Whatever it is that you wish to discuss with him will have to wait."

"Listen, you don't understand. If Philip doesn't see me now, I will take this money and business elsewhere. This is serious."

She hesitated for a moment before she reluctantly picked up the phone and dialed his extension on it. She removed it from her ear after a moment. "He's not answering," she said and got up. Loon guessed she was headed to the office and followed her.

They were almost there when the door opened and a man who must have been Phil stepped out of it.

"Rissa, what's going on? Who's this young man?" He asked, wrinkling his brows at Loon.

Marissa turned around swiftly, but not as swiftly as Loon, who brought out his gun and waved it at both of them.

Phil slowly put his hands in the air.

"What the hell is going on?" Marissa whimpered in response.

"Where's Kim? Tell me right now, or I will shoot you both. Trust me, I will not hesitate," Loon said ominously, pointing the gun back and between the two of them. "Tell me where she is right the fuck now!" He shouted.

Phil cowered slightly, his hands still in the air in surrender. "Okay, man. Calm down. She's inside my office."

Loon nodded, taking a glance at the door. "Open it," he commanded. "Let me see her right now."

Phil turned back and opened it. He looked at Loon, who pointed his gun at his head. "Go on in, both of you," he said, using his hand to push Marissa in. They opened the second door and Kim gasped when she saw them. When Loon pushed through the door, he knocked her down.

"Hey, are you okay?"

She nodded. "Yeah."

He helped her up.

Out of the corner of his eye, he noticed Phil take off rushing towards his desk.

He dashed towards him and grabbed his arm. "Don't even think about it. Back the fuck off."

Phil raised his hands up.

Loon pointed the gun at him and slowly walked backwards, he checked the desk Phil was aiming for. Opening the second drawer, he saw a 9mm gun under some files. He took it and tucked it in his waistline.

Still pointing the gun at Phil, he ran back to Kim.

"Loon," she breathed out.

"Hey, listen to me. I just overheard those guys who were looking for you earlier. This man..." he paused. "Is somehow connected to your parents' murder."

"What are you talking about?" Phil asked, faking innocence.

Without indecision, Kim grabbed the second gun tucked into Loon's belt and pointed it at Phil, her hands shaking. "You killed my parents?" She asked with a weak voice.

"Kim, baby, I had nothing to do with that. Your

parents were like a family to me. I would never..." his voice broke down.

"Then how did you know about the puppy? Only momma, Jason, and I did," she said. "You had to be in my house when all this shit happened or you had it done."

Phil laughed. He tried so hard to make it casual, but it still came off as awkward. "Well, I guess... you know I heard you a couple of times talk about you wanted a puppy, so I assumed..." he trailed off.

Loon and Kim looked at him questionably.

"Go on," she said.

Phil chuckled and moved forward a little bit. "Come on, Kim. Why are you doing this? You know you're like a daughter to me," he chuckled again as if he couldn't believe what was happening. "I would never..."

"Hey!" Loon yelled. "Don't try that emotional blackmail shit with her."

"Tell me the truth Phil," Kim said.

Phil's face dropped. "Alright. Your father was being a bit of a nuisance to some very powerful people, Kim, so he had to go. I had no other choice. You and your mother weren't supposed to be home," he admitted, reluctantly.

Out of shock from his confession, Kim fired a bullet at his thigh and he yelled painfully and dropped down. Marissa yelled out a panicked cry too and Loon looked at Kim, surprised.

"Give that to me," he said reaching his hand out for the gun.

She ignored him. "If that was the case, why were you

trying to sex traffic me then, Uncle? You're fucking *sick*," she said, gritting her teeth to emphasize the last word.

Phil grimaced in pain. "There's this powerful Israeli drug Lord, Ezra Kapon. He was your father's business partner," he panted, struggling to put words together. "He offered 800k for you, I just couldn't resist."

"You're lying. Daddy's business partners barely know me," said Kim.

Phil was using his hand to apply pressure to the wound. "He had your family under surveillance when he first got into business with your dad. They ran guns and drugs up and down the coast using the Bella cargo trucks. He wanted to make sure he could trust him. During that time, he came across videos and pictures of you and he's been fascinated with you ever since. He's the one that's sick and the one you need to worry about. He wants so desperately to have you."

Kim stared blankly at him, trying to decipher everything he just said. Her parents were murdered by the person they trusted the most in this world. No one deserved that.

His breath became more rapid and shallow. "Can I get an ambulance, please?"

All this time their worst enemy is literally so close to them. How could he? How heartless you gotta be to do that to people who considered you to be family?

Kimberly's dad and Phil got tight after Phil's son, Philip Jr. was found dead under a freeway overpass in Emeryville in 2006. Phil was just the man to oversee her father's finances, but they bonded over Philip Jr's murder because of Kim's older brother, Dominic, who was also killed just 2 months prior.

Phil's voice brought her back from her trance. "I wasn't really going to go through with it, you know. But he's as smart as he is dangerous. So, I had to make it look convincing. I was going to arrange a fake death for you so you could escape and... uh, start a new life somewhere. I had it all planned out," he chuckled wryly.

Kim kept quiet for a moment before she burst out in pained laughter. "I'm not buying that, and you know it. So, why don't you give me access to all of daddy's bank accounts instead?"

"I... I don't have it," he stammered an answer.

She shot him again, in the arm this time. "Daddy's accounts. Right now!" She demanded.

Phil cried out. "I don't have it. I only have a little over half of it in a safe at my house," he shivered.

Kim looked at Loon and he nodded, but before any of them could do anything else, the door burst open, making Kim and Marissa jump.

15

Three armed security men stood, ready to fire. Loon quickly grabbed Marissa by her hair and put a gun to her head, holding her hostage. Kim did the same trying to stick close to Loon's side. "If you try anything, I'm going to shoot her," she said. "Dead this time."

Loon realized Kim was all-in to push the line to get the answers she wants. The security men lowered their guns.

"That's right. Now back off," said Loon. They slowly started making their way out, Loon and Kim made for the door, with Marissa still at gun point.

"You idiots! Don't let them out of this building!" Phil shouted, panting. "Shoot them!"

The men seemed hesitant, as they kept glancing at Marissa. "Sir, what about..."

"I will replace her. Fucking shoot them!" Phil yelled again. The men were tentative, but soon followed his order and started firing shots.

It began raining bullets.

"Shit!" Loon cursed. They bent down and ran out of the room, with Kim dragging Marissa. The security followed on their heels, and one of them shot again. The bullets trailed them as they ran to the elevator and hastily pushed themselves inside. The security men turned around to take the stairs.

"Oh, my God!" Kim panted.

The elevator opened and they rushed out. They heard the security men yelling and Kim glanced back, staggered. "What the hell, they've already descended?"

"I would say so," answered Loon.

They ran out of the building and made it to the car. A sharp pain hit Loon's side, followed by a warm trickle and a numbing feeling. He glanced down and saw the trail of blood as he walked. A patch of red stained his clothes and quickly ruined the leather seats when he got in, but the seats were the least of his problems. Everything around him was starting to slow down.

"You're wounded," Kim stifled a gasp. She could see through the gaping wound, and the blood bothered her. She quickly pulled out the cigarette lighter.

Loon was still panting when she came closer.

"Wait, what are you?"

His eyes widened when she burned the wound with the lighter. It hissed as the heat burned his flesh, but the sound was overwhelmed by his scream which soon trailed off as his eyes rolled inwards and he passed out. She sped up and drove them far enough until they got to an out-of-service gas station, where she parked behind.

Loon opened his eyes just as the car was stopping.

Loon saw Marissa through the rearview mirror. She looked like she had been betrayed and he didn't blame her. Phil was a bitch ass nigga.

————

Loon knew that now would be the perfect time to get information out of Merissa. She'd been betrayed, and that look of disbelief on her face said it all.

"Hey, receptionist lady. Tell us about Phil's safe. And don't lie. I know you got the info," he said still a bit hazy from the pain.

Marissa didn't look up. "There's one at his house and one at his mistress' apartment hidden behind the refrigerator... or stove... I think."

"Smooth."

"The one at his house is hidden behind his bathroom mirror," she added, looking down.

"Hope you know the passcodes," said Kim. "Give Loon the codes and the address, we'll drop you off and go straight to the mistress'."

Loon cleared his throat and said, "You do know after this, you'll have to get as far away from Phil as possible, right?"

Kim chuckled and Marissa nodded. When she got out the SUV and gave Loon a piece of paper with the address and passcode on it and the two sped off.

· · ·

Loon parked in the driveway of the apartment and got out of the car.

Loon checked the call box on the apartment. Irene Nikaido was listed there. It was a small unit with only two tenets.

"Should we call her?" Kim suggested.

Loon pursed his lips. "You for real, shorty?"

"See if she'll answer," she added.

Loon shrugged. "Okay, I guess." He pressed #002 to Irene's apartment. It rang twice then went straight to voicemail.

"Yeah, I don't think she's home," he concluded.

Kim frowned a little. "How will we get in now?"

"Beat you to it," she heard Loon say, door wide open.

Her eyes mirrored it. "How did you do that?"

He flung a tiny metal between his fingers. "A little friend. Always comes in handy," he said, then put it back on his ring. It fit in like a glove and if he hadn't done that in front of her, Kim would never have been able to tell there was something attached to it. Damn.

Loon crept in and Kim quickly followed his lead.

"Where is it?" She asked, scanning around, with her hands on her waist.

Loon pointed to the kitchen. "There. Behind the fridge."

They walked to it, and Loon pulled the fridge out. The safe was there like Marissa had told them, Loon used his hands to open the cover door to the safe and began typing the code. The first code he entered blinked 'wrong' but the second one worked, which meant the other code must be for the safe at Phil's house.

"Whoa!" exclaimed Kim, as she was pulling out wads. "There's more than a mil in here. We'll need a bag or something." She paused and pouted. "'Money can look like a lot until you count it,'" she quoted, smiling.

Loon smiled a little too. "That's right."

"Still. We're gonna need a bag." She quickly stood up, only to come back moments later with a Fendi duffel bag.

"Here. Let's use this," she said.

"Where did you find that?" asked a surprised Loon.

"In her room. Come on."

They tossed all the money inside the bag and then closed the safe back.

Loon started to push the fridge back but first opened it looking for something to drink. A Brita water pitcher caught his eye and he took it out, instantly draining the contents into his mouth.

He noticed the way Kim was looking at him. "What?" He asked.

"Nothing," she said looking like she was trying hard to conceal a smirk.

They were on the way out when they heard someone attempting to open the door. "Goddamit!" cussed Loon.

"Quick. Let's get in there," Kim whispered, pointing at the hallway laundry closet.

The door opened and a sexy drop-dead gorgeous Asian chick with hair dropping below her waist walked in. She was talking on the phone as she walked right past the refrigerator and moved to the center of the kitchen without noticing anything.

Kim breathed out a sigh of relief and grinned at Loon.

16

Irene ended the call and walked into her bedroom, leaving the door halfway open. She went into her closet for a pair of clothes to change into and immediately noticed her Fendi duffle bag wasn't there. She brought half of the closet down, looking for it but still couldn't find it. She gave up and decided to undress. Loon could see Irene through the cracks in the laundry closet door.

"Oh, my God! Are you looking?" Kim teased in a whisper and he smiled slightly, taking his eyes off. They were waiting for the perfect time to sneak out.

"Hey, did you perhaps take my Fendi duffel yesterday?" They heard Irene asking whoever was on the other end of the phone. Loon looked down at the bag and they both cackled.

"Keyara, if you have it, it's cool, just bring it back tomorrow." She paused a bit. "Cause you are the one who's always running off with my stuff. Just... just bring it back."

A moment later, Irene came into her living room in a t-shirt and panties and flung herself on the couch, turning on the television, which was on a news channel reporting about a shooting in the financial district. Loon and Kim looked at each other wide-eyed. The news was about them.

Irene made her way to the kitchen to get a glass of wine and stopped abruptly, surprised to see her refrigerator sticking out further than usual. She shrugged, grabbed a bottle and a glass, and came back to the living room. She picked her phone up again and dialed a number.

"Hey babe," she smiled.

"Irene, this Mike," a voice answered.

"Oh hey, can I speak with him?" She asked.

"Irene, sorry, Phil's in the ER. We at Kaiser right now, he was shot." Mike said.

"Oh, my God!" exclaimed Irene, looking at the television.

"Is there anything I can help you with, Irene?" He asked.

"No. no, it's fine, I guess. I just wanted to ask why the fridge was moved. I'm on my way down there. I have to make sure he's okay."

———

Mike hung up without a word and ran into the ER trying to force his way to where Phil was.

"Excuse me, sir, you can't be here," a nurse told him.

"It's urgent," said Mike.

"Let him in," Phil strained, clenching his jaw.

The nurses reluctantly backed off and Mike rushed inside. "Miss Irene just called, Phil. She said it looks like the fridge had been moved and I think..." he trailed off.

Phil cursed and jumped out of the bed ripping his bandages in the process. The nurses gasped. He could care less about the look of horror on their faces or the pain in his body. He grabbed the phone from Mike and called Irene back.

She picked up on the first ring. "Hey."

"Irene, it's me. It's Philip," he said.

"Oh, my God, Phil! Are you okay? I'm on my way down there, I just saw on the news..."

Phil interrupted. "No. Stay put. I'll be. Do me a favor and check the safe right now."

"Okay, give me a moment while I check." She said and paused for a while. "Holy crap! The safe is empty, babe!" She screamed when she came back to the phone.

"I need you to tell me the truth, Irene. Have you told anyone about the safe?" Phil asked.

"Of course not. Why would I do that?"

Phil took in a sharp breath. "Stay put. I'm sending Mike over there," he hung up and turned to Mike. "I need you to investigate what happened and get my money back. Whatever it takes," he commanded.

Back at Irene's house, Loon cursed, realizing Phil's guy will be showing up any moment now. He looked at Kim and nodded, she nodded back and they both stepped out of the laundry closet at the same time.

"What the hell?" Irene said when she saw them. She tried to run back into her room, but Loon grabbed her. She struggled to break free, screaming and kicking.

"Shut up!" Kim shouted. "We're not here to hurt you, lady. But if you continue screaming, well then we will have to shut you up."

The news is still playing on the TV as the breaking news comes on.

"A body was found inside a dumpster in the financial district, only a few blocks away from where the shootings took place. The body was recognized to be that of Marissa Hernandez from Daily City. Currently, the Police are not sure if there is a connection to the shootings, but are looking for Luis Johnson and Kimberly Bell for questioning." reported the woman.

"Son of a bitch," said Loon.

Kim's face fell. "He killed her," she stated. "And now, he's framing us for it."

Loon nodded. "Kim, go to the kitchen and see if you can find duct tape or something to keep her quiet."

She walked off and came back less than a minute later. "Here," she handed it to him.

"You people are crazy. Phil will find you," Irene said, no doubt realizing what they were going to do.

"Yeah okay," answered Loon casually. Together, he and Kim ducted tape Irene's mouth, arms, and legs and locked her in the bathroom.

"Now we go for the safe in his house?" Kim suggested after they were done.

Loon shook his head. "Nah, I don't think that's a good idea. But we could make Irene call Phil and tell him about us, that way he'll send all his people here, leaving his house unguarded for sure," he smirked.

They went into the bathroom and Kim gave Irene her phone. "Here you go. Call Phil, tell him we're here and we are gonna kill you as payback for Kim's parents."

"You two are crazy," she said.

Loon rolled his eyes. "Yeah, you said that before. Now make the damn call."

Kim nudged her temple with her gun to motivate her a little bit.

Irene gave Loon the eye, clearly thinking he was the weak link since he was a guy, but it didn't work. He pointed his gun right next to Kim's, even brushing her hair in the process.

Irene sighed and finally dialed the number. "Babe, babe they're here. The two from the news. They said they're gonna kill me because of something about Kim's parents. Hurry, come quick. I'm afraid to die."

"Better get a move on, Uncle!" Kim yelled in the background.

Then yanked the phone away from Irene and put the tape back over her mouth before she could say anything more. They hurriedly walked out of the apartment and hopped in the car quickly and sped off.

Before leaving the block, Kim glanced back and saw

three cars already turning into Irene's driveway. She laughed. "Shit."

———

When Loon and Kim got to Phil's house they climbed over the gate and quickly ran across the huge lawn.

"There," Kim pointed at a window. "It's the kitchen. There's a way in."

They were able to get in through the kitchen window, with Kim almost injuring her leg when it snagged against the frame and she'd fallen forward. Loon had caught her in his arms and helped her down.

"Easy," he whispered.

They stepped out of the kitchen and into the lounge and a dog quickly ran in to play.

Kim snickered. "This asshole really has my dog." She took the pup in her arm and started smooching it.

"Um, we should get this over with and get out of here ASAP. He'll soon figure out it was a trick," Loon said.

"You're right," sighed Kim. She put the dog down, and it followed closely behind Loon as they headed to the master bedroom straight to the bathroom.

Nothing was there.

"That bitch!" Kim almost shouted. "She lied to us."

"Not necessarily," Loon said, realization hitting him. "She stated that it was in the bathroom but didn't specifically say *which* bathroom."

Kim nodded slowly, taking it in. "You're right... again."

"Yeah. I mean, this is kinda a big house. How many rooms are there? We gotta check all of them."

And so they did. All 4 of them, but nothing was there.

They reached the end of the hallway and there were no more rooms.

"Either she lied to us or Phil changed the location not long ago," Kim was saying.

Loon leaned on the wall mirror. He opened his mouth to say something but a sudden clacking sound stopped him.

He stood straight, alarmed.

"What was that?" Kim asked, looking around frantically.

Loon noticed a bright sliver of light coming out of a tiny slit behind the mirror. Instinctively, he placed his hand on it and pulled.

It opened up like a door.

"Where did that come from?" Kim asked looking. "Whoa."

They walked into what looked like a sex dungeon. The all-black leather furniture gave the place a certain atmosphere—she wasn't sure what it was, but it was sort of dark and curious. A stripper pole stood in the center of the room, with cages and swings and several massage benches. Kim's attention was hooked when she saw a wall with an assortment of whips and chains. Mirrors covered the floor to the ceiling, sending out reflections all around.

"Damn. Phil," said Loon, smiling a little. "Uncle Phil a freak."

Kim opened her mouth to respond but was speechless.

They had a hard time finding the safe. It was perfectly hidden behind a Kara Walker painting on the wall.

Loon was admiring the work when they found it. Kim recognized it as her father's. He kept it in his office. She figured Phil must've taken it after he had her parents killed. She declared to take it back. She yanked it a little too forcefully and when it came off, a piece of wood wall split off as well.

"Wait, is that…?"

"I think that's the safe," Loon snickered, pointing at the little metal appearing from behind the wall through the tiny hole Kim made when she yanked the painting.

Loon pushed around the area and finally heard a click. Then a section of the wall popped open exposing a safe behind it. He tried the second security code Marissa gave them and it instantly opened to reveal tons of money, jewelry, documents, and photos all piled together.

"God! This is huge. We'll definitely need something to pack this all in," said Kim.

"I'm gonna go check the bedroom," Loon offered.

He rushed upstairs and grabbed a black suitcase from the side drawer in what must have been Phil's side of the closet. On his way out, he subconsciously noticed a picture of Phil in the hallway. He was standing next to some guy and Congresswoman Rebecca Townsend who's currently in the running for Vice President. He returned with the luggage.

"Here, this will do," he said to Kim, who nodded. They quickly shove everything from the safe into it.

"Great. Now, grab the painting and come on," Loon said.

She stopped to scoop up the pup as well, smiling at the lil fella. "This is also mines."

17

Mike and his team arrived at Irene's apartment and kicked the door open. They entered the house, guns in hands.

"Shh. Sweep the apartment. Find Irene," he whispered to them. He looked towards the refrigerator and tightened his lips. He went over to investigate it. It wasn't broken into, it was opened... with the passcode. *So, this wasn't a theft. The person who did it must have had the knowledge of...*

"Here she is, Boss," the boys interrupted his thoughts. They had walked in with a duct-taped exhausted Irene.

Mike nodded. "Untie her." He called Phil and put in on speaker. "We found her, Phil."

"Irene," Phil's worried voice called out.

"Philip," Irene sobbed.

"I'm so sorry, baby. Can you tell me exactly what happened?" He asked.

"Yeah," she sniffed. "They made me call you. Said I

should tell you they were gonna kill me, and then... then they left shortly after. They were the ones who took the money."

Phil paused a bit. "How many of them? Can you tell me what they looked like?"

"Two. A man and a woman, both were black. The woman had short dark hair, the man had long braided hair."

"Oh, fuck! Kim," Phil breathed. "It was Kim, Mike. Right now, it's possible they are going for the safe at my house. You need to get there. Fast!"

"Yes, sir. On it," said Mike. He ended the call and they rushed out, leaving a few guys behind to keep an eye on Irene.

They sped off to the house and once they arrived, they burst in the door, heading straight for the safe, only to find it wide open... and again empty. Mike ran his hand over his waved hair, aggravated, and called Phil once again.

"Yes, Mike. Tell me," he said immediately.

"I'm sorry, sir, but this safe is also empty," Mike said.

Phil shouted in rage, kicking his legs over to the side of the hospital bed and swirling painfully on the bed. He stood up and began throwing things on the floor and breaking them. Nurses and security rushed in to subdue him.

Phil pushed them off him and made his way to the door. They ran and grabbed him again. He kept struggling, trying to break free until a doctor walked in with a syringe and quickly pushed it into Phil's arm.

"No! Don't..." he couldn't finish the sentence. Once sedated the nurses put him back in bed.

Meanwhile, Loon and Kim, were in the car, parked on a corner between two black cars, under a busted lamp post. Loon brought out his phone and dialed a number.

"My ex, Robyn works at the Wade Regency Hotel. She might be able to plug us with a spot to lay low for the night," he explained to Kim, who nodded.

"Hey," he greeted when Robyn answered the phone. "It's Loon."

"Loony?" Robyn asked amazed.

He chuckled. "Yeah. So, check this out, I need a favor."

"Anything for you, baby," she said.

"Can you get me a room on the low? And I would need to come in through that VIP entrance you used to tell me about. It has no camera access, right?"

"Right," she answered. "No public access also."

"Perfect," said Loon.

"I'll text you the room number, and leave the door cracked open for you. The card key will be under the pillow. That good?"

"Better than. Thanks, Rob."

"You are welcome," she said and hung up.

A message popped up with the room number after barely a minute and Loon started the car.

———

Kim asked Loon to stop by Jason's house before heading to the hotel.

"I need to drop off the dog," she explained a little distantly.

"Sure," he agreed. "Want me to come with?" He asked after they got to the house.

She held the dog carefully and shook her head. "I'm good."

Jason answered the door, and his face sagged a bit when he saw Kim.

"Uh, hey," he greeted her awkwardly, his eyes moving to the dog and then back to her. "What's up?"

"Just wanna drop this off," she responded and handed the dog over. Jason was still unsure about what was happening. The expression on his face was questioning.

"I'm going to explain everything later," Kim promised, asking him to take care of the dog for a little while.

"Oh, you seen your uncle then?" Jason mentioned to Kim just as she was about to leave, holding the dog to himself.

She frowned, pondering on the question, but went back to the car. Once inside, it hit her. Jason had mentioned Phil, but how did he know Phil had her dog? There was only one way that was possible.

———

They drove to Wade Regency and went in through the VIP as planned. The security there asked for their names, and when he found them in his registry, he let them through. They entered the elevator and arrived at their floor seconds later. Loon and Kim headed straight through to Room 1915.

The door was cracked just as Robyn said it would be. "Wow, she *is* good," said Kim.

They walked in only to find her lying across the bed naked.

"Huh?" Kim tilted her head.

Loon blinked. "Robyn."

She quickly sat up, dragging her clothes to cover her body. "Loon. Um..." she trailed off.

Kim burst out laughing and Robyn blushed.

"Who is that?" She asked. "I thought you wanted to have fun... for old time's sake."

"Oh. Oh, this is Kim. Kim, Robyn," Loon introduced.

"Nice to meet you, Robyn." said Kim, still smiling.

"She's just a friend. We have some business we need to take care of though... privately," said Loon.

Robyn's face fell. "Oh, well." She stood up from the bed and quickly put her clothes back on. She stopped in front of Kim, eyeing her up and down. "You know," she bit her lip. "The three of us could have a little fun."

Kim raised a brow.

Loon guided Robyn towards the door. "Sorry, Robyn. But it really is strictly business over here."

"Then I guess I'll see you later," she said after a pause.

Loon handed her a wad of cash from the Fendi duffle bag. "You will. A little something for you. As I said, this business is private."

Robyn beamed. "I get it," she collected the money and turned to walk out. Loon couldn't resist smacking her as she walked off.

Robyn glowed.

Kim broke out laughing again as soon as the door closed behind Robyn. "Play on, player," she teased.

He blushed. "That's not... not what it looked like. I'm getting married in a few months and I've been faithful."

"Uh-huh," she sassed. "So, what's the plan, player?"

18

The tall walls, that endless pitch of darkness, and the loud screeching noise. *They're* back, Kimberly thought, turning away on her heels. Upon reaching the door, Caleb and Asher's faces appeared and she realized the laughter was coming from both of them, as they chorused, echoing the empty room. She crouched and placed her hands on her ears, screaming. After some time, Kimberly slowly raised her head and saw herself in the lounge back home. Caleb was dragging her Mom out as she shouted, for them to let her down. Her voice was soon drowned by the chilling screams of her mom getting dragged all the way out the door.

Caleb was bellowing. Kimberly stood up to go after them, but her head hit a wall, she looked up gritting, but Caleb stood there with his heavily built body, smirking down at her. She instantly moved back and fell on the floor, she started moving backwards slowly, as he approached her. *"What do you say before we send you off*

I give you the sex of a lifetime? Personally, I enjoy taking it from women. So feel free to fight me," he said, giggling like a maniac. Suddenly, she was at the kitchen counter, she picked up a knife and slit her wrist, and watched the blood rushing out of it. She woke up in a hospital bed and felt a rushing anger when she realized she wasn't dead.

Kimberly found herself sneaking through the hallways and elevator until she was on the hospital's rooftop. Everything played out in a blur. She closed her eyes and took a deep breath, then let go and was soon flying down —falling and falling and falling, till her body hit the charcoal road and her brain burst open. A piercing pain bolted through her bones and her head swimming in the pool of her own blood. Noises and screams echoed around her.

"Oh, my God! Is she dead?" a woman asked.

"She must be dead. Her head is literally ripped open," a male voice answered.

Kimberly's eyes started closing. She must be dead' that's right, so why isn't she? She tried moving her limb, but she couldn't, her body had become numb, yet she could feel every single pain coursing through her veins as she felt tears rolling down her eyes.

Loon, on the other hand, was woken up by Kim's tossing and talking in her sleep. *She must be having a terrible dream,* he thought. He sat up, squinting his eyes. Kim was shivering, sweat all over her body.

"Must be dead," she kept mumbling, over and over.

She must be having a nightmare, he thought, sitting down on the bed. "Kim," he called.

"Must be dead," she mumbled again.

He shook her. "Hey, Kim. Kim, wake up!" He shook her a bit harder, and she woke up and started violently attacking him. "Whoa, whoa!" said Loon, grabbing her hand that was punching his chest.

"Leave me alone! Get away from me!" She yelled, scratching out at his eyes. Something her Grandma taught a few years ago.

"Kim, hey. It's me. It's Loon," he told her, and she looked up with her teary eyes.

Her hands slowly fell and she sighed, looking down. She was panting and her hands were shaking, Loon noticed. He reached in to hug her and she broke into tears.

"It's okay, it was just a dream. It's okay," said Loon.

"It was so realistic. I was... I was dying," she cried out. "The rape... my parents... I... I..." she trailed off.

"Shh, shh. You're safe now. I won't let anything happen to you," assured Loon. "I promise."

Kim's eyes adjusted to the sunrise coming in from the window. She could see a complete view of it from right there in Loon's arms. It was so beautiful.

With the rising sun and the amazing view of the city, the room had kind of made her feel better. Plus being in Loon's arms, she realized it might not be all bad.

After a moment, she fell back asleep in his arms, and he drifted off too shortly after, still holding her. He woke up first and tried to sneak out the bed, without waking her up, but his movement woke her. Kim reached over and grabbed his hands, then yanked him back down. The gesture took him by surprise and he fell on the bed next to her. He opened his mouth to talk, but somehow, the way she was looking at him, staring into his eyes, made him stop. She slowly inched her body closer and just as slowly, placed her mouth on his, enveloping his lips in a warm sensual kiss. Loon was stunned for a moment, taken aback.

"Kiss me," she said, amidst entangled lips. When he still didn't move, she broke the kiss and raised her eyes at him. "I want this," she declared.

"No," he said, unclenching her hands. He wasn't sure she was in the right headspace and wasn't about to take advantage of her.

As if she had read his mind, she said, "You won't be taking advantage of me. Trust me, I'm okay."

He didn't budge.

"I want this," she repeated, pulling him closer and this time, Loon kissed her back, he couldn't control it anymore.

Kim got on top of him, and as they kissed she removed her clothes and helped him remove his. He flipped her over and was now on top of her, kissing her harder. He gasped as he broke apart and reached for her bosom. She helped him remove her bra and he reached for her nipples, gently sucking on one and massaging the other. She directed his hand to her middle, he followed her lead and soon his finger was inside her. And he struck. In and out and in and out.

With every thrust, he took her breath away.

She grabbed his head and pulled him closer, eating up his lips.

The way it all flows naturally shocked Loon.

He felt like kissing her forever. Like their lips were made to just... connect.

Damn.

She expertly reached for his boxers and pulled them down with his help.

"Oh wow," she laughed. "Oh, that's big."

He laughed too. Couldn't say anything. Really there's nothing to say. If you're blessed you're just that... blessed. He went back for her mouth.

"So soft," he murmured and she chuckled.

Gently, she grabbed his cock and just as gently started to stroke the shaft. Loon stopped kissing her and moaned so loudly, it made her laugh.

He just realized he has actually wanted this from the moment he saw her in that bathroom back in the motel.

Loon was eager to be inside her but she wouldn't let him. The thought still terrified her. Sure, she felt safe with him but painful memories from the rape flashed through her mind. A part of her wanted him badly, but the images in her mind repulsed her and made it hard.

His touches and kisses kept them at bay, and she wanted to loosen up and let him in, but what if the whole experience sucked? What if she let her thoughts screw things up, and everything became awkward afterwards? The more she thought about it, the harder everything became. *Just don't overthink this,* she thought to herself.

Loon's voice pulled her back.

"Please," he breathed out arching his hips.

She kept kissing him and slowly stroking his shaft. Just when he was about to cum, she let go.

Loon almost swallowed his breath. The look on his face made her giggle.

Wicked.

She got on her knees in front of him and he quickly parted his legs. She held his cock and gently shoved it inside her mouth. Loon literally let out a cry. *Why does this feel so fucking good?*

In just a few seconds, he exploded. Right into her mouth. She didn't push away. Not even once.

When he was done, she cleaned her lips with the back of her hand and just sat back, looking at him.

"Now?" He asked, panting. He couldn't wait anymore. He might die if he didn't get inside her in the next 10 seconds.

Kim smirked. "No."

"Please," he demanded. "Please."

She pretended to ponder over it. "Okay," she said after a moment. "Think we can make that work."

Loon grabbed her lips with hunger as if he couldn't stand being away from them.

She took a hold of his cock and gently guided him to her sex where a damp paradise welcomed him. She winced and held his arms desperately when he penetrated fully.

Hmm, she's tight, he thought.

She bit her lips and tapped his arm when he started moving in and out.

"Are you okay?" He asked with concern.

"I just need to breathe," she said. "It's... it's my first time."

"That explains the hesitation," Loon said with a smile. She nodded slowly and averted her gaze. Sure, let him think that.

"I'll take it slow," he promised and kissed her.

The pain was sharp at first, but as he began to move steadily it shifted into something pleasurable, and she was soon holding him tight and moaning, the pain now a pulsating heat spreading through her body.

He moaned louder than he has ever moaned before. He had never felt this way before in his entire life.

It was everything.

Loon wanted her.

All of her.

Minutes later, he lay down on the bed facing up, trying to catch his breath, and as the sun came up, he knew he had just had the sex of a lifetime.

"That was... incredible," he confessed.

She giggled.

"Was your first time as good as you expected?" He turned to her and asked.

Her smile was shy as she nodded, "Better than expected."

Loon furrowed his brow, "Am I an asshole for feeling

something I've never felt with Jess?" He wondered out loud. He always thought they could get there at some point but the comfort he felt with Kim seemed organic.

"Well, what made you want to marry her in the first place?" Kim asked.

It was at that moment he realized he never really connected with Jessica in an intimate way like he just had with Kim. She was just hot, freaky, and pretty much stroked his ego whenever he needed it. There was no real substance to their relationship. Feeling bad for the way he was starting to look at his relationship with Jessica, he decided to clear something up for them both.

"I'm still going to get her out of this shit. I got her into this mess. It's my job to at least make sure she's safe," he said.

"Of course," said Kim.

"But I still want to figure out what's this between us," he added, almost absent-mindedly. "And anyway." Clears throat. "You have what's his name... J... Jason?"

A thick awkward air swooped past them. Kim didn't say a word.

He cleared his throat again. "So, what's our next move?" He asked, mentally putting together a list of hustlers that owe him money. It was time to collect. He decided to write it down on a notepad he found by the bedside table. He had come up with 12 people but there were 3 on the list that owed the most and a collection from them would set him up nice financially. Cap, Scooter, and KG.

"Cap should be the one we hit up first," Loon said.

"He owns a car dealership that served as a front for his large distribution network. We were childhood buddies, so I'm guessing I'll get the least pushback from him. And since I don't have my usual 'team, I need to approach with a soft respectful touch... sorta."

Kim shrugged, "Well, let's go then."

Damn, she looked really good. Loon swallowed, unable to take his eyes off her naked body, and the hypnotic sway of her ass. He watched as she walked across the hotel room to the bathroom, then a throb between his legs caught his attention and he smiled.

"Yeah. Let's get it."

19

Loon and Kim walked into Cap's upscale dealership. "This place is disgusting," said Kim. Loon chuckled as a young lady walked up to them.

"Hi, I'm Charlie. What car are ya'll interested in?"

"Damn," Kim said almost subconsciously.

Loon frowned. "What?"

She pointed at something and his eyes followed her hand. She was pointing at a 2024 Mercedes-Benz G-Class with black with red trim.

"I want that car."

Loon raised a brow.

"Oh that is a wonderful choice," the lady started to say beamingly. "The Mercedes..."

Loon interrupted. "Hey. Hey. Sorry. Uh, we need to speak with Cap. He around somewhere?" He said, touching Kim's hand a little to remind her what they were there for.

Her face fell a bit, "In that case, I'm sorry. He isn't taking walk-in meetings today."

"Right," he nodded. "Well, I insist that you tell him about me anyway. Loon. Loon Johnson is the name."

Her nostrils flared. "Fine," she turned around and strode off to make a call. Cap picked up on the fourth ring.

"What, Charlie?" He asked, lazily.

"Someone's here to see you. Loon Johnson. I told him you weren't seeing anyone, but he insisted," she told him.

"Mmm," he said and hung up.

Soon after, three heavily built guys came out from the back office. They stopped in front of Loon and the one standing in the middle glaring at Loon asked, "What business do you have with Cap?"

Loon chuckled lightly. "Not your problem, man. But if it's all the same to you, I would like to discuss it with Cap privately."

The guy smirked and tilted his head. "Get rid of him," he said, but quicker than fast, Kim had the barrow of her gun pushed directly at their leader's dick.

"Shiiit!" One of the guys cussed.

"Back up! Back up!" The leader yelled.

Suddenly, a speaker went off and Cap's voice filled the showroom. "Hey, hey, hey. Now that's not how we treat old friends, Stace. That's my nigga Loon from way back," he paused a little bit. "Charlie, show Mr. Johnson up."

Stace glared at them. "This ain't over, nigga. Yo bitch, no one gone save you next time."

Kim put her gun down, as she glared back at him. They followed Charlie up the stairs to the office where Cap was. The whole walk up Loon couldn't help but notice Charlie had a very curvy figure like Jess and he found his eyes lingering on her small waist and fat ass.

Kim noticed and snickered. "Really, nigga?" She asked in a whisper.

"Gun at his dick? Really?" He asked back.

She laughed and he joined her. They reached the office and there stood Cap, at the door, to greet them like the old friends they are.

"Ahh," he dragged, hugging Loon. "Loony. What's been up, my nigga? How you been? Hey, sorry about all that, bro. Didn't know it was you."

Knowing that was some bullshit because he heard Charlie tell Cap it was him. Loon just smiled. "It's good, G."

"Well, who's the fierce pretty lady you with, man?" Cap asked.

"His down ass bitch," said Kim, before Loon could talk.

He looked at her, surprised, but was quick to regain his composure and he laughed it off casually. "That's right. She is."

"She's amazing. It's always good to have a good one by your side," said Cap.

"Ha-ha. Thanks," Loon said and Cap invited them in.

They sat down on the sofas and Cap told Charlie to make them some coffee. The office wasn't like Loon imagined it would be. He had never been in there before. It had large one-way windows overlooking the showroom floor, a massage table in the corner, and the smell of incense burning wafted through the air. Some slow jazz was playing softly.

"Cap, are you selling cars or spa memberships?" Loon teased.

Cap threw his head back and laughed. "Well, a man gotta make himself comfortable in his space right?" He spread his hands. "I like my space."

Loon nodded. "I can see that."

Cap laughed again a little, then quickly got serious. "I've been hearing rumors, man. That you skipped town to hide because you owe some major players out in Israel?"

Loon nodded. "Yeah. I didn't really skip town to hide, but yeah. I do owe someone big money. I just need to get low so I could figure shit out and plot my next moves to make things right.

Cap nodded, understandably, as Charlie walked back in with a tray. "I get it," said Cap.

"Matter fact, that's why I'm here," he paused to say thanks to Charlie and picked up the cup. "That 375k, I kinda need it. No, I really need it, like yesterday."

Cap stared at him for a while, before he broke up laughing. Loon joined him after a sip or two of his coffee.

"Well see, the thing is Loony, I can't give you that right now," Cap told him.

Loon raised his brow. He put his cup down and inclined forward on his chair. He tightened his lips.

"Cap, do you remember the favor I did for your nephew when he was scared for his life in the county? I had two of my C.O.'s who were on my payroll and my crew looking out for him," he shrugged. "I never taxed you for it."

Cap opened his mouth to speak but closed it and sighed. "You're right. The truth is, I really don't have that money with me right now. The most I will be able to come up with on this short notice is $150,000, maybe $175,000."

"Well, figure it out, man. Cause I really need that money," Loon said.

Cap looked like he was contemplating for a while. "Alright. Why don't you take one of the luxury Lincoln Navigator SUVs? I got three of them fully loaded and you could easily get $70,000 to $80,000 for each."

"I ain't here to Craigslist a fucking car right now, nigga!" Loon yelled.

Cap narrowed his eyes. Loon sure seemed bold for a desperate guy. "Look, it's all I got and I think you should just..." his tone was starting to get icy and Loon didn't appreciate that. He cut him off, his voice harder.

"I might be down right now, but you know my track record. When I get back on top—and trust me, I fucking will... I'll crush your world."

Cap knew Loon's reputation alright, so he lost the hardness and raised up his hands in defense. "I'm sorry, man. But really, that's all I got. You could pick whichever you want. If you could wait a few more days though, I could get the rest of the money."

Loon nodded. "Okay. I'll wait. And I'll also take a car."

"Well, walk down and just take your pick," beamed Cap.

"Nah, I don't care. Just make sure it has a full tank of gas," Loon said.

"Okay," he said and called Charlie back up.

She walked in, "Sir."

"Get the keys to the blacked-out Navigator on the floor," he commanded and whispered something in her ear when Loon turned to talk with Kim.

Loon nodded at him. "Nah. Let me get that G Wagon on the showroom floor."

Cap chuckled nervously. "Er... Loony, I don't think..."

"This isn't a negotiation, Cap. I'm taking the G Wagon."

Reluctantly, Cap nodded. "Okay."

Kim couldn't hide her excitement. The squeeze she kept giving his hand told him that.

"How much do you think we could get for it?" He asked Cap.

Cap shrugged, looking displeased still. "$100 to $130k. $150 if you find a sucka."

20

Loon and Kim pulled up in front of Evergreen Cemetery. He glanced at Kim, she had a scared look on her face all of a sudden, "You okay?" He asked, worried.

"Yeah," she said, quickly regaining her composure. "Let's do this."

"Okay. Help me grab the mixed bouquet from the backseat," said Loon.

Kim turned around. "Remind me why we got flowers again?"

"Because Scoot is still affected by his mother's passing and this is a quaint but easy way to show both of them respect."

Kim nodded understandably.

They got out the car and entered the cold and silent cemetery. After a couple of steps, they heard snaps of small branches and both quickly spun around. Two sturdily built men stood there. The shorter one had a mustache moved forward and paused directly in front of them.

He scoffed. "You Loon?"

Loon cleared his throat. "Um, yeah."

The taller one looked them up and down starting with Loon then Kim and then nodded at his partner. "Follow us," he said.

They made a turn and walked for about 5 more minutes, before arriving at the grave. Scooter's Mom's grave. They could smell the scent of burning sage on top of the tombstone. Scooter always held meetings there, for some reason. His mother was a big-time Drug Lord in the 70s, Loon thinks Scooter feels like she guides him. The thought made him shiver internally.

"Loon," Scoot nodded at him. He was down on his knees as if praying or talking to his mother. He had his head bowed down and when he talked, he didn't look up. A dozen of boys stood behind him. "Search them," he added to the boys without waiting for Loon to answer his greeting.

Loon snickered as the men held him. "Seriously, Scoot?" He asked, unbelievably.

Scoot hesitantly looked up and tightened his lip, "Give me a second to finish talking with Mama."

Loon nodded. "Of course."

After like two minutes, Scoot gently touched the stone and stood up. His lip twisted into a fake smile. He shook his head at the boys and they stepped away from them.

Scooter walked forward. He studied Loon and Kim

with probing eyes, and he grinned. "I haven't seen you in a long time, Loony," he said and reached in for a hug. He nodded at Kim and shook her hand. "Scooter. Nice to meet you."

"Kim. Nice to meet you too," she said.

Loon took the flowers from her and gave them to Scooter. The man collected the flowers smilingly and nodded at Loon to show he appreciated the respect he showed his mother.

"That had to be done, sorry. Don't know if you've changed, don't wanna find out the hard way" said Scooter, laughing. "I heard your club got knocked," teased Scooter.

Loon furrowed his brows. That situation caused him to lose three of his guys, he wasn't gonna joke about it with Scoot the Comedian. "Since you obviously have been keeping up with the news on me, you know why I am here. I need that paper I'm owed," he told him.

Scooter glanced at his boys and they all threw their heads back and laughed hard. Loon looked around, confused. Scooter finally stopped laughing. "Sorry. I'm sorry, but what you talking 'bout, *money you're owed?* What are you owed, Loon?" He stepped back and rested his hand on the tombstone. "You ain't got no muscle with you, Loony. I could bury you along with your pretty bitch right here in one of those open graves over there." Pointing to the roped off area to their left.

On hearing that, Loon quickly reached for his guns and Kimberly followed suit. They stood like that glaring at each other. Scooter's guys were stepping in closer, looking back and forth between the three of them as if they were predators waiting for a signal to pounce. It was an awkwardly scary moment.

But suddenly, Scooter began to laugh again. "Come on, dawg. I was just playing around with y'all, man. C'mon bro, you know we go way back. I already knew what you wanted and why you called." He reached behind the tombstone and pulled out a duffel bag. He walked over to Loon and unzipped it, showing him the contents. "See? Relax. That's $175,000 I owe, plus another $50,000 for letting a nigga slide for so long."

Relieved, Loon and Kim put their guns away. "You play too much," he said, collecting the bag. Scooter jumped to sit on top of the tombstone, smiling. Just then, Scooter notices a caravan of black SUVs speeding inside the cemetery, heading right in their direction

Scooter's eyes widened. "The fuck, Loon? You line a nigga up, bruh?" He asked, pointing a gun at them.

Loon glanced back at the SUVs. "No... Scoot. No, I didn't. I don't know what's going on. Real talk, fam."

Before anyone could do anything, the invaders parked the car carelessly directly in front of them and started hopping out. It was Philip and his crew. Phil was walking with a cane now.

Kim made a loud screech and pulled out her gun, pointing it directly at Phil. "What the fuck are you doing here?"

"How did you know where we were?" Loon asked the more pressing question.

Phil merely shrugged with a smirk plastered across

his face. "Your fat friend Cap gave you up. For $100,000. Worth every cent."

"That's not possible. He didn't know we were coming here," Loon said and sighed when the realization hit him. Cap put a tracker on the Benz. That punk bitch. "Damn it!" He cussed.

Phil started moving towards them and Kim shouted. "Stay back! Stay back, you psychotic sadistic maniac, or I'll shoot you I swear. And this time I'mma make sure you die."

Phil's smirk was intact. He looked at Loon. "Look, I don't want any trouble. Just give me the pain in the ass girl and we can be on our way," he looked around at the graves. "After all, you know there are dead people here, right?"

"I'm not going anywhere with you," said Kim.

"We'll see about that."

Scooter cleared his throat. "I'm sorry, what the fuck is going on?"

"This got nothing to do with you, young man. It's a sad coincidence that they happen to be with you at the moment. I just need the money this little bitch stole from me."

"Stole?" Kim asked, tilting her head to the side unbelievably. "You robbed and murdered my parents for that money, you asshole."

Scooter squinted his eyes, surveying them. Kim and Loon were clearly outmanned. Outnumbered and outmaneuvered by Phil and his guys, he decided to back Loon up by pointing his gun at Phil too. His boys followed suit.

Altogether, they were twice as much as the number of Phil's men.

Phil smiled. "I told you this has nothing to do with you, didn't I? You wanna be in so bad?"

Scoot shrugged. "Well, who doesn't want a little bit of fun and excitement? I'm not letting this go down on my watch. Loon good with me."

The standoff between the two crews lasted for almost ten minutes before Phil backed down and put his gun down. He tightened his lips and gestured to his guys. They all fell back and headed back towards their SVUs. Phil turned around to glare at Kim one more time. Scooter lowered his gun with a sigh.

"Look. I don't know who that guy is or what exactly went on between you two, but I think you need some more protection... and a place to lay low for now."

Loon nodded. "Yeah, that's probably a good idea."

"Nasir, D, and Mark, you three stay with them," commanded Scooter.

21

Philip hit the steering wheel in fury and glanced back. "Find everything you can about that Loon guy."

One of the guys nodded. "Yes, boss."

"We need something we can use to our advantage. Make him back off from Kimberly," Phil added.

"What's he even doing with her?" One of the guys wondered out loud.

Another snickered. "Wasn't it obvious? They fuckin."

Phil ignored the comment and picked up his phone. He dialed Ezra Kapon's personal phone number. He picked it up on the third ring.

"It was about time I hear from you," Ezra said, in that cold husky voice that always sent a chill down Phil's spine.

Phil chuckled nervously. "Yeah."

Phil's restless voice alarmed him. "What happened?" Ezra asked.

"Um..." he cleared his throat.

"What?!"

Phil sighed helplessly. "I lost the girl, Mr. Kapon."

Phil could hear him breaking something in rage and that made his heart skip a beat. "She ran off with some save a ho ass nigga. We found them, but they had some pretty strong backup."

"So, now she knows you're involved?"

"I'm afraid so," said Phil.

"What the hell? How could you be so reckless? You promised me everything will be executed perfectly," Ezra said.

"I'm sorry. She slipped away. The situation was getting loud and messy. We had to pull back but I'm on it. It's just a temporary setback."

"Well, you better find her. Otherwise, I swear to you. You and your family will kiss this world goodbye," Ezra threatened.

Phil swallowed. "You know, Ezra... I could ship you way badder girls by tomorrow."

"I. Want. Her!" said Ezra, gritting his teeth. "I've been fantasizing about her ever since we met 17 years ago. If your boys weren't dumb enough to kill Steven and his wife without securing access to their accounts, we wouldn't be here right now. They left the money to her and she'll only get full access to it once she turns 25. Now, I need her for that account and then I'll force her to marry me. Do you understand?"

"Yes, Ezra. I will... I will get her. I promise," Phil said.

"Make it fast, my friend. I don't want a bullet to get between us," said Ezra.

Phil chuckled nervously, scratching the back of his neck. "It wouldn't, Ezra. I promise, I'm in the process of getting info on her bodyguard now." Phil said.

"Who is he?"

"Some random street dude, I presume. He's not new to this that's for sure" answered Phil.

"Alright, I'll get Meir to help. He knows all the players in the game. He'll get in touch," Ezra said and hung up.

Phil caught his breath and sighed. He felt anxious and nauseous. Talking to Ezra did that to him all the time. He knows he wasn't bluffing when he said he would kill his family. Although they've been sort of friends—mostly alliances—for the past decade, Ezra wouldn't blink twice before putting a bullet in Phil's head if he doesn't get what he wants.

Phil finally arrived at Irene's apartment. Irene calmed down a bit as she offered him a seat, smiling.

"Got something to drink?" Phil asked. His throat felt so dry and needed something to take his mind off Ezra's death threat.

"Sure," said Irene. She went into the kitchen and came back moments after, Myscellan Cognac and a glass in hand.

"So..." she started. "How did it go?"

"Badly," said Phil. "I couldn't get the girl. That guy, Loon, and his friend were protecting her."

"Well, what do you want with her anyway?" She asked.

He shrugged. "Just some money. And then I'll ship her off to Israel. Got a good deal on that one," he said, grinning widely.

"You trafficking her," Irene stated, rather than ask.

"Yeah," he said casually, pouring himself another shot.

Irene shook her head. "What the-Are you crazy?"

He looked up at her. "Babe, I..."

"What, you going to traffic me too someday?" She interrupted.

"What? No. Of course not. What are you saying?"

"Don't do it," she said, clenching her jaws. "And if you do, then just know that it's over between us."

Phil almost choked on his drink. "Babe, come on. It's not trafficking in the dark way you're thinking. I just need her to get me some money out of an account in Israel. That's all."

She shook her head, standing up. "I don't believe you."

He chuckled dryly, "Why?"

"You do all sorts of nefarious things. I know you. You're lying to me and you really are planning to engage in human trafficking," she said, glaring at him.

He put his cup down and stood up. "Babe," he touched her shoulder. "I just need her to get me the money, that's all. I promise you."

Irene yanked her shoulder away. "Then, why are you so pressed to find her? And why is she running like that?

Why'd they come here, and most importantly why did they do that to me?" She was on the verge of tears.

Phil sighed. "She's trying to steal from me, babe, that's why she's running. You saw how they already took all that money in here. And I'm sorry," he took her hand and looked her in the eye. "I'm so sorry you had to go through that because of me, but babe... I promise you, I ain't trafficking no one."

Irene stood there, still glaring.

"You need to trust me, Irene. Please! I'm not gonna hurt that bitch. She's the one who hurt you, and because you have such a good heart, you still standing up for her."

Irene looked like she was gonna say something, but just sighed and shook her head. "Okay."

"You believe me?"

"For now," she replied, with a light smile.

She went to her room and came back out moments later. Phil had sat down and was on his 4th shot. Irene burned a sage and lit up a few candles, creating a relaxing atmosphere. She has always been heavily into crystals and astrology. She pulled Phil back on the couch and removed his shoes.

"Babe, no. I need another shot," he protested.

"No, what you need, my love," she said. "It's a massage." She began pressing gently at his neck and shoulders.

Phil moaned. "Yeah, that feels good."

"Mm, it does, doesn't it?" She chuckled and bent her head down to his ear. "You know what, why don't you call Detective Steigerwald? I bet he could find a lot of dirt on that guy," she whispered.

Phil falling deep in the massage remembered Loon and Kim are wanted right now by the Police for the murder of his assistant Marissa. He could use this to get Loon out the way.

Irene started moving the massage down his chest and reached her hand inside his pants. "If you found them once, you will find them again," she said, still whispering in his ear, wording it so it felt like his idea.

"I could immediately tell the detectives where they are when I do," Phil said, his voice sounding distant.

He realized that once the two are in custody, he could have them hand over Kim, making it look like she escaped arrest and Loon would stay there. Phil felt good about his plan and was sure it was gonna work. He gently pulled Irene over to him and reached in for a deep passionate kiss. He lifted her dress and had her bend over the couch. She gasped when his hand slid up her thighs, and soon the sounds became soft moans pulsing through the air. He grunted and thrusted hard into her, his body pounding against hers while he pulled her arms back and held her firm. Her moans became sharper and her cries for him to go deep filled the air. He obliged.

Right after they climaxed, he fell to the couch, drained. Irene giggled, passing him his phone. "Here. Call him," she said, panting. Phil nodded and grabbed the phone from her. He dialed Steigerwald's number.

"Hi, Mr. Hart," the polished detective greeted in his strong accent.

"Hello, Detective. How is work at the station?" Phil asked.

"It's good. How can I help you?"

"Can you meet me down at my office later today?"

There was a little pause before Steigerwald said, "Just say whatever you got to say over the phone, Mr. Hart. This line is secure." He never really cared for Phil. Always thought he was slimy and has been tolerating him only because he paid well.

"Fuck it. I'm on my way to your station," Phil said and hung up before Steigerwald could react.

Ezra calmly complemented the beauty of the estate they just walked into. He nodded slowly, impressed, and walked up to the front door with three of his goons. Six of his men stayed in the front, securing the area, while the rest walked around the back. Ezra was as calm as can be, exhuming power and authority with each step he took.

He locked his hands in front of him after ringing the doorbell. The sound echoed inside the house and he waited, his goons flanked around his side looking as stiff and grim as they could be. The calmness in Ezra's eyes quickly gave way to an impatient flicker when he picked up the door knocker and slammed it several times.

Stopping only when a few footsteps drew close to the door, Ezra waited. A voice boomed from inside.

"Don't open that door!"

It came a little too late and the oversized door opened. Ezra's eyes became fixed on the young girl at the door, eyeing her nubile body over. He flashed a devilish grin at her.

"What's your name?"

The young girl looked at him and then the other men, and then her eyes back on him.

"Kimberly," she replied a bit hesitantly.

"That's a beautiful name, and I'm not surprised because you are such a beauty. You have pretty long hair..." he paused and took a step closer, lowering his voice. "I've always loved a young lady with long hair like yours."

Kimberly smiled.

"Ah, and then there's that wonderful smile," Ezra continued, his eyes moving from her lips to her smooth neck and lower.

Steven appeared at the door and glared at Kimberly. "I told you not to open the door," he scolded her.

"But I..."

He cut in impatiently. "Never open the door to strangers. I'm not sure how many times I'm gonna have to hammer that into you."

Kimberly lowered her head.

"Hey, cut the little girl some slack," Ezra intervened and Steven finally acknowledged his presence with a hard stare. Ezra was unmoved by it, exhibiting a calmness only a man in charge could wield.

Steven introduced himself to Ezra, still standing at the edge of the front door—almost like a vampire waiting for an invitation to walk in—and his smile was back when he noticed the slight change in Steven's demeanor; the worry creeping in.

"Don't worry, there's nothing to worry about," he assured Steven while offering what was supposed to be a friendly smile but was just as unsettling as getting a greeting from a guy with a gun. Steven's eyes were on Ezra's goons, so he assured him that his boys were fine.

"I always drop in on people I consider doing business with."

Steven's eyebrows fused and he froze for a moment. A car honked somewhere in the distance and drove past, and for the past three minutes, the heavy barking of a dog had carried in the direction of the house, blown in by the crisp air.

Ezra broke the silence. "Can I come in?"

Steven hesitated, rubbing his dry fingers and once again staring at those other guys uneasily. He nodded and Ezra stepped in with a bright smile.

"You have a beautiful home," he complimented Steven while glancing around at the place. He turned to Steven, "A lucky man you are; you have a beautiful daughter and such a beautiful home. I always admire men with eyes for the finer things, if you know what I'm talking about."

Steven gritted his teeth and exhaled slowly.

Ezra rubbed his hands together and lifted a brow. "I just complimented your house, I think you can be a gentleman and acknowledge that."

Something told Steven this man talking about being a gentleman was anything but that.

"Thanks," he mumbled and Ezra shrugged.

Both men looked in the direction of the hallway when Kimbella walked in.

"What's going on? I heard voices and..." she stopped when her eyes met Ezra's, then shot a questioning gaze at Steven.

"And yet another beauty in this house," Ezra chuckled and wagged a finger at Steven. "Eyes for the finer things."

He went on to introduce himself to Kimbella, almost courteous.

"Fix me a drink, will you?" He ordered and Kimbella's eyes became set.

She pinched her lips and once again glanced at Steven for some sort of explanation. Ezra could only smile when he saw that shocked expression on the woman's face; he could almost imagine the words screaming out to her man.

"I'll take a double of whatever alcohol you have," he broke their silent communication and walked around the house. Kimbella walked away, tight-lipped and uneasy. Steven would have some explaining to do.

"Ooh," he pursed his lips and smiled when he set eyes on a rich leather chair in the main living room. He settled himself on it and sighed satisfactorily. Steven was saying something about that being his favorite chair but Ezra cut in and said, business-like, "You were recommended by my people in San Jose."

Steven walked over cautiously, saying nothing.

"I heard you own the second largest tow truck

company in Northern California, quite impressive." He paused and gazed at Kimbella when she came in with a glass of vodka.

Ezra gestured for the coffee table by his side and watched with wide eyes while she bent over and placed the glass on the table. Steven clenched his fist when he saw the way the man looked at his wife. When Ezra glanced at Steven, he had a smug look on his face; almost as if he could feel Steven's quiet, almost helpless, rage building up.

He raised the glass to his face and took a sniff of the clear liquid, the sharp smell fizzling up his nostrils.

"Not a vodka man," he said and placed his lips on the glass, doing everything deliberately. A long sip and he winced and gulped down the liquid. "But I never shy away from something hot. Now, back to business," he cleared his throat, still holding the glass in his right hand.

The rings on his fingers glistened, and the silence around him was almost awed. "Despite owning the second largest tow truck company, you still managed to be in large debt due to your addiction to gambling and high-end hookers." He shook his head and a sly smile crept onto his face. "You're a bad boy." He paused after that and watched Steven's eyes twitch at the horror of having his secret revealed, and also the shocked expression on his wife's face. Ezra was laying his cards out carefully and confidently; he was in charge of the game.

Sitting up, the rich leather chair crunching, he cleared his throat again and broke down his vision.

"I've got nineteen trucks covering northern California. Now, the plan is to have your trucks transport my merchandise in the towed vehicles. You'll get to handle small money pickups through fake dispatched calls. My people will call in asking for a tow and say, 'Please come expeditiously', that's important because it's going to be code for a money pick up."

His words rolled out smoothly and carefully, hanging onto the silence around him. Knowing that Ezra obviously knew things about him, Steven tried to cut in and interrupt Ezra. Sure, Kimbella knew he had some money problems but not to the magnitude this guy was revealing. He caught Kimbella's gaze and knew it was already too late. She stormed out of the room.

Fuck! He cursed quietly and was about to go after her when Ezra's goons stepped in his path, grim faces and all.

The glass clinked softly on the coffee table and Ezra faced Steven.

"You can fix your marriage later; we're not done discussing business." He said this matter-of-factly, without giving room for any argument. Steven glared at him but Ezra flicked it off; he might as well be the owner of the house. His eyes became hard now and his calmness fizzled out. "That," he warned, pointing in the direction Kimbella had stormed off into. "Should never be a reason for you to cross me. You have to think this over before committing to it because once you're in there's no turning back."

The warning was clear and Steven wondered if he truly had any other options.

Ezra caught Kimberly walking into the next room,

while Steven remained in deep thought, rolling over the offer in his head. He stared at her sitting cross-legged on the floor, her skirt riding up her smooth legs.

Very nice, he thought and imagined entering the room and having more than a few private moments with her. *I wonder what she has under that tiny skirt of hers,* his wild thoughts went on. *Probably something cute and sexy.* He wanted to run his hand up her skirt and eat her out. The thoughts were inappropriate given how young she was, but he didn't give a fuck.

"Well..." Steven began to give his answer, but Ezra held a hand up, interrupting him. He stood up and adjusted his shirt.

"I'll expect an answer tomorrow. One doesn't just make a hasty decision when it comes to business now, am I right?" He chuckled but Steven kept a straight face. "Talk it over with your beautiful wife."

Steven grunted.

"Kimberly," Ezra called out and the young girl appeared at her door. He smiled at her and winked, "See you later."

"Do not speak to my daughter!" Steven warned, stepping over to Ezra, pointing a finger threateningly in his face.

It didn't sit well with Ezra, who snarled and pushed the hand out of his face.

"You better watch how you talk to me," he responded harshly.

Kimbella was standing by the porch smoking a cigarette when Ezra walked out. She heard the footsteps but kept her eyes forward, puffing out clouds of smoke from her pursed lips.

She froze when Ezra stopped beside her.

"You're gorgeous," he whispered with that sly smile. "I'm looking forward to our future relationship."

She recoiled when a hand dropped on the small of her back and moved towards her ass.

"Fuck off!" She snapped and pushed away, slamming the door behind her.

23

"I need you to find everything you can about a guy named Loon," Phil said sitting on Steigerwald's desk inside the station.

Steigerwald looked like he was pissed that Phil just showed up to the station the way he did, but he was trying hard to hold on to his composure.

He cleared his throat. "Uh, Mr. Philip, can you please get up from my desk and sit on the seat?"

Phil shook his head. "Nah. The dirt I have on you allows me to sit wherever the hell I want."

Steigwarwald sighed. "Okay, fine. Suit yourself."

"So," Phil leaned in. "I want to find this punk name Loon. I think his last name is Johnson"

"Loon? Loon wanted in connection to the murder of Merissa Cannes?" Steigerwald asked.

"Yes! Yes, that Loon," he said.

"Why are you looking for information on a guy that is

wanted for murder, Mr. Philip?" Steigerwald asked again, slightly getting annoyed.

"It's a long story, Steigerwald. But I need it ASAP."

Steigerwald sighed. "The department has been looking for him and the girl too. Three days now, and found nothing. I'm sure even if I look, I won't find anything useful to either one of us."

"Listen, Steigerwald, I could help you catch this guy if I can get all the information I can on him. In return, I just want the girl. Imagine what bringing him in could do for your career. I smell a promotion," Phil told him.

Steigerwald chuckled lightly. The little annoying prick had his attention. He was getting to him. "Only thing I know is that he has a girlfriend, her name is Jessica Townsend, but when cops questioned her she said she hasn't seen him in days. We have cops tailing her just in case, but Phil, I don't think Loon will be popping up anytime soon."

"Why's that?" Phil asked.

"Well, we've been onto her for two days now. From what we found, she has been laid up with some Israeli dude, er... Lyor Avi, I think that's his name. A known heavyweight associate of kingpin Meir Kapon. Ezra Kapon's nephew."

Phil nodded. He took the investigation papers that were on the desk and handed an envelope over to the detective. "10 stacks. No need to count it," he said.

Steigerwald looked at the envelope and then at Phil's face. "Do not forget our agreement. You call me the minute you find them."

Phil smirked. "You got it, Steig."

They shook hands and Phil walks out of the station. He got in his car feeling a little bit better than he did earlier. He gave one of his guys the investigation papers. "Lyor Avi. His address is written there. That's where we are heading."

The guy nodded. "Yes, boss."

———

They pulled up to Lyor's house in front of his large iron gate. Before they could do anything, several shots were fired at them.

"Shit!" cussed Phil. "Get down."

"Who the fuck are you guys?!" Someone yelled through an intercom from the house.

"I'm Phil Hart!" He yelled back. "I come in peace. I just want to talk about some business concerning a mutual enemy."

"Who?"

"Luis Loon Johnson."

There was a short silence before the voice sighed. "Come in. Alone. Just you."

Phil sighed, looking at his boys. "I guess I'll have to do this alone."

"Boss," one of them said. "I don't think it's a smart move to go in there alone. That guy sounds crazy."

"Yeah, well," he opened the door. "I have to do it." He walked towards the house with his shirt lifted and his hands up, showing he had no weapons on him.

The electronic door slowly swung open. Two security men led him up to the house. They knocked and Lyor himself opened the door.

"Have you frisked him?" He asked the boys without sparing Phil so much as a glance.

They shook their heads no and immediately started searching him. Phil gritted his teeth and tried to keep in mind it was all worth the big payoff in the end.

The guys nodded at Lyor who smiled. "Take a seat," he said.

The men exit the house.

"Make yourself comfortable. Do you want anything to drink?" Lyor asked.

"No, thank you," chuckled Phil.

Lyor shrugged and sat down beside him. "Okay."

"So, I heard you have an entanglement with Loon Johnson's fiancée, Jessica. Wondered if she knows or is willing to provide a way to get in touch with him," he said.

Lyor's eyes widened. "How'd you know that?"

Phil shrugged, nodding his head. "Let's just say I have my connections inside the OPD that keeps me informed. You can use the source too if you help me find Loon."

"No, thank you. Me and my crew already got some insiders on payroll at the moment." He paused a little. "I'll still help you find Loon though. I would like him out of the way as much as you do."

Phil nodded. "Great then. Let's get to it."

"Mmm. Now, what would I get out of the deal?" Lyor asked.

"50 grand just for the help. Anything else you need?"

He nodded. "I need Loon completely out of the picture. I want to be able to send flowers to his funeral service next week. You feel me?"

"I promise. Long as I get what I need from him, I will kill the boy," Phil told Lyor.

Lyor grinned widely. "Good. Good. That's what I like to hear." He shook Phil's hand.

Lyor picked up the landline and called up to their bedroom. He whispered something Phil didn't hear and a few minutes later, Jessica came walking out the bedroom in nothing but lingerie. She loved showing off her body to whoever was around to see and Lyor never objected to that.

She walked gracefully to where they sat. "Hey," she said to no one in particular. Lyor kissed her lightly on the cheek. "Call Loon from the burner phone," he said.

"What?" She asked with furrowed brows.

"Yeah. Call him," Lyor repeated.

She slowly sat down. "Er, haha. Are you sure? My fake kidnapping was supposed to stay in play until Meir got all the money from Loon and then you can kill..."

"Shut up!" Lyor yelled, cutting her off. "Shut your damn mouth, bitch. We don't even know this nigga and you out her telling my shit. Just go do what I tell you. Tell him you're still a hostage but one of the guys guarding you slipped up and dropped his phone."

Jess nodded frantically. "Okay."

"Tell him you think you might be able to get away next time they let you out to shower or use the bathroom but you need to know how to find him first so you can know where to go from there."

"Got it," she said.

"Show me," Lyor said.

Phil nodded at the idea.

Jessica acted out what she was going to say as if preparing for a movie role until Phil and Lyor were satisfied. Then she finally dialed Loon's number.

24

Loon and Kim, along with Scooter's boys got in the car to go see KG. Loon picked up his phone and dialed Cap's number. He didn't pick up, so he decided to leave him a voicemail.

"Hey Cap, this Loon you bitch ass nigga. I just wanna tell you that what you did... how you played us, it wasn't cool bruh, but it's all good. Payback's a bitch and you should be expecting her," he said.

They arrived at KG's BBQ Grill & Bar and parked outside. Loon walked to the counter, and a guy who looked strikingly familiar asked, "What can I get you?"

"Nothing, thanks. We are here to see KG," Loon said.

The guy reluctantly nodded, glancing at the boys standing behind Loon. He came from behind the counter and walked them to where KG was. When KG saw Loon, he sighed.

"What up, man?" Loon greeted.

"Look, Loony. All I can do right now is 80k and you'll have to take it or leave it," KG said.

Loon snickered. He couldn't believe it. "Fuck you talking about? How the fuck you gon' be making me an offer on what I'm owed? You think I'm some collection agency or some shit, my nigga?"

A wave of tension swept the room as the boys on both sides looked more than ready for war to pop off at any second.

It was the most intense standoff Loon has ever been a part of, and that pissed him off. Plus, the betrayal and backstabbing from Cap. He's not taking shit lightly regarding the money that was owed to him. Cap fucked it up for everybody,

Guns raised and were pointed. Eyes fixed at one another with glares that if looks could kill, Loon is sure they would have all fallen dead right that very second.

Nobody moved. Just more stares.

"Look, Loon," KG said again. "I'm not your enemy."

"You are if you trying not to pay me what you owe," Loon told him.

His phone rang abruptly and Loon glanced at it confused. He stepped back a bit from the standoff and picked it up.

"Loon, baby," he heard her panicked voice.

His heart skipped a beat. "Jess?" He asked.

"Yes. Loon," she laughed weakly, probably at how surprised he sounded, but it was quickly drowned by the quiver in her voice. "Loon, I—"

"Jess, hey, hey. I can hear you. Where are you, Jess?"

"I... I don't know," she said sounding even more scared.

"It's so good to hear from you, Jess. How are you calling me?"

"Um, one of the guys dropped his phone earlier before they went out," she said, her voice quivering. "Listen, Loon. I think I can escape, but... I don't have much time. Tell me where you are so I can try to come meet you. Please, Loon. I'm scared, I don't know what they will do when they come back. I need to get out as... soon... as possible."

"Okay, calm down, Jess. You'll get out of there," he looked at Kim. "Take the money. We're leaving."

Kim pursed her lips, confused. "I don't think we should back down. We need to get the rest of it."

Loon glared at her coldly. "Do as I say," he said through gritted teeth.

"But Loon..."

Loon slapped his palm on the phone. "Grab the damn thing and let's go!" He yelled.

Kim furrowed her brows, irritated and scared at the same time as she stooped down and picked up the bag.

"This ain't over!" Loon yelled at KG as they walked out.

Loon and Kim got in the car with the boys confused as ever. They wondered why Loon just backed off from their standoff. They began murmuring amongst each other.

"Can you people please shut the fuck up? I'm on a call," said Loon. "Listen, Jess. I'm currently staying at

Scooter's stash house in North Oakland over off 60th and Whitney. It's the blue crib with the white Benz wagon in the driveway. Can you hear me?"

Jessica was silent for a moment. "Er... yes. Yes, baby. I can try to get there. Thank you. I think someone's here. I gotta go."

"Okay," he said. "Jess?"

"Yeah," she answered.

"Come back to me," Loon said.

"Yeah. Yeah, I will," she said, hanging up.

Loon dropped the phone. "That was my fiancée, Jessica. She said she thinks she can get out. She'll come meet us at Scoots. We need to get there right now."

Kim didn't spare him a glance throughout the whole ride back to Scooters. He knew she was upset at him for the way he yelled at her in front of everyone so he decided to explain himself.

He sighed. "Look. I'm sorry. Jess was saying she can get away. The major point of gathering all this bread is to get enough to pay off Meir so he can let her go. But if she can get out, I wouldn't need to pay him shit. Since he crossed the line, fuck him! I'd just need to body him. And if that's the case, why risk a war with KG if I don't need to?"

Kim's shoulders fell back a little showing she understood but she was still a little pissed. Loon held her hand up to his mouth and kissed it. "I'm sorry."

She pulled her hand back and folded her arms.

Loon smiled and tried to look at her but she glanced

away. He playfully waved his right hand in her front again, but she looked away.

She nodded, still not looking at him. "It's okay." She felt like she had to say it, but was it truly okay? *Just ignore it*, she told herself but the thought of losing Loon only made her sad.

They got to the house and Loon quickly got out of the car. He stopped dead in his tracks as he stepped into the house. "Remember that guy that was working by the counter at KG BBQ Grill? The one who took us to KG?"

The boys nodded. "Yeah."

"That was KG Jr. I just remembered where I knew the boy from," he said. "I need ya'll to go back there and snatch him up. We need leverage in order to make his daddy pay up the remaining 220k, plus another 50 for the inconvenience."

"Yes, sir," one of them said. They turned around to leave.

"Do not hurt the kid. But don't leave without either the money or signed papers to the ownership of the grill."

The silence following the departure of his men made him realize that he was all alone with Kim. *Maybe I shouldn't have sent all my guys off on a mission*, he thought and his gaze strayed to Kim. A part of him felt he should be okay until they got back, although he wonder if that would be the case.

Kim leaned against the wall looking at him as he eagerly awaits another phone call from Jessica. She was glad that Jessica was getting out safely and escaping her kidnappers, but she was worried about how it may affect her and Loon's new relationship. She hadn't felt what she did with him for a while and probably never had. Not even with Jason and she's scared she to lose that.

"Hey," Loon said grabbing her waist. "What you thinking?"

"Er, nothing," she said feeling those butterflies she always did whenever he'd touched her.

"You're thinking about what will happen if Jessica comes back, aren't you?" He asked, dipping his head in her neck. "Hey. I've realized I am not *in* love with Jess, but I feel responsible for getting her in the situation. I only want to see her back safely."

"Are you sure?" She asked. The doubt weighed down her voice. Somehow, she couldn't get herself to believe that he'd ultimately choose her over Jessica, and the thought nagged at her. This wasn't how she hoped it'd end.

She was silent for a while, her thoughts straying far, punctuated by heavy sighs.

Loon leaned in and kissed her, pulling her attention back to him. "I've never been more sure about anything in my life. I can't just start something with you and not see where it goes."

Suddenly the loud sounds of multiple vehicles pulling up outside interrupt them. Loon looked out the window and it was Phil and his crew.

"Shit!" He said. "It's Phil. We need to get the guns." They scrambled to gather them from where they were hidden under some floorboard under the couch.

"Damn it! How the hell did he even find us? I thought we tossed out the tracker," Loon said.

"I don't know," said Kim, just as confused. "Maybe... maybe he overheard Jessica's conversation. I hate to say this Loon, but she's probably not coming."

Someone pounded on the door three times. "Come on, Loon! We just want to talk," a voice said.

"Wait. That's not Phil," Kim said.

Loon tilted his brows. He thought he recognized the voice too but wasn't sure. He peeked out the window and was surprised to see who it was at the door.

25

It was Lyor Avi. Loon signaled to Kim to keep quiet as he moved to the door and looked through the peephole. "What you doing here, Lyor?" He asked, still surprised to see him.

"Loon!" Lyor also tried to peep. "Loony. Listen, man, Philip and I are only here to talk and things will go super smoothly if you just send that bitch outside."

Loon closed his eyes, clenching his jaw. Phil just wouldn't give up.

"What do you have to do with any of this, Lyor? And where the hell is Jess? Is she with y'all?"

"Nah," Lyor shook his head. "But don't you worry about her, she's back at my crib cooking dinner in her panties."

"I'm talking about Jessica, my fiancée."

"I know who you're talking about, fool," said Lyor.

"Fuck!" Loon cussed. Jess had been caught. "What'd you do to her?"

The man threw his head back and laughed hard. "What did I do to her? Nothing! You got played, silly nigga. She's my bitch now. Always been my bitch."

Loon shook his head frantically. "No," Kim tried to hold his hand, but he yanked it away. "You're lying. You're lying!" He yelled.

A few fumbling sounds, then audio started playing through the door. It was the sound of two people having sex, no doubt.

"Hear that?" Lyor said.

"Yeah, but it could be you fucking your own Mama for all I know. I can barely hear shit from in here," said Loon.

Lyor laughed. "Oh yeah?" he asked, pressing his phone. "What's this then?" he pushed the phone through the mail slot.

Loon hadn't recognized his fiancée's moaning sounds, but when he took the phone, he saw it really was a sex tape of Lyor and Jessica.

Furious, he threw the phone on the floor, causing its screen to crack.

"Ooh, somebody's big mad," Lyor said and they all laughed.

"This is not real. You raped her, you fucking perv!" Loon drew out his gun and started shooting through the peephole.

Lyor, who was taken by surprise, got shot in his arm. He raised his gun and started shooting at the glass window with his other arm.

"Get down!" Loon yelled at Kimberly. He bent down behind a couch, changing his clip.

"You scared little bitch!" shouted Lyor, amidst shootings. "You thought you were invincible, didn't you, Loony? Well, look at you now. A lame bitch ass nigga."

"Is that what this is about, Lyor? You got jealous of me?" Loon snickered.

"Keep Jess. I don't want that bitch anymore. I got what I wanted from her, and guess what? I got it first. So enjoy my crumbs." He fired shots at the now-half-open windows.

"Lyor!" Phil yelled at him. "Stop! You might kill the girl. We need her alive, otherwise, Ezra will have us both killed."

Lyor ignored him and continued shooting. What Loon had said really set him off. He never really liked the guy, always pretentious, always condescending. *He thinks he is better than everybody*. All Lyor wanted was to collect everything Loon has and then kill him in the most horrible way possible. He laughed, "That's all you got, Loon? Pay closer attention to the video. Jessie was enjoying herself. Listen to the way she is moaning and calling out my name. Hell, she was never yours to begin with, and even if she was, well guess what? I got your bitch and I'm making her feel more than you ever did."

Kim glanced at Loon to see his reaction. He was clearly boiling with anger, with jaws and fists clenched.

"Tell me, Loon. You ever fucked her in her ass?" Lyor continued. "Oh, Jessie! The things that bitch makes me do. You know, just this morning before calling you, she was fucking me. She loves to be in control, doesn't she? That little slut," he laughed.

Unbeknownst to both of them, Philly and his boys had snuck in through the back door. Before he could do anything, Loon saw them in front of him.

He quickly reached for his gun.

"Uh-uh. Put it down," Phil said.

Loon did as he was told. Kim, however, had her gun pointed at Phil. He laughed. "Put it down, Kim." She refused to. "Put it down, or lover boy here dies."

Kim frowned. There were at least 6 guns pointed at Loon, and there was no escaping this. So she did the only thing she could think of.

She cocked the gun placing it under her chin with her finger on the trigger.

Phil merely laughed. "What are you doing?"

"I'll pull the trigger if you don't let him go this instant," she said, tears falling down her cheeks. "I mean it, Phil. I know you need me alive. I'll pull the trigger."

Phil started moving forward, hands up. "Now now, Kim. It's fine. You don't have to do that. Here, I'll let him go."

Kim moved back a little.

Phil slowly moved forward. "I promise you." He turned back. "You can go."

Kim's eyes wandered off to look at Loon, and Phil used that opportunity to seize the gun from her, ripping it out of her hands.

"Attagirl," he smiled and crawled to the window. "Fall back, Lyor! We got them."

"Huh?" Lyor said.

"They're restrained. Come on in, I've opened the door." Phil said and walked over to Kim, grabbing her.

"No! Loon!" She yelled, but Phil's guys had held Loon back. He struggled to break free and the boys beat him down hard. Loon fell to the floor and when he tried to get up, they knocked him back to his knees.

Lyor entered the house, beaming. He gave Loon a wink and laughed, feeling totally pleased with himself, then he cocked his gun at him.

"Oh yeah. I've been waiting for this day," he said.

Phil shook his head. "Not now, Lyor. We still need him alive for now."

Lyor frowned a little but then threw his head back and laughed right after. "Oh, Loony! How I've waited for this day, Loony. You have no idea," he put his gun down and crouched in front of Loon. "You have no idea how much I hate you, Loon. You and Meir," he grimaced. "Everything from the beginning to this moment was planned by me, you hear me? Everything. Even you meeting Jess, your club being raided, you being chased by the feds. Took me years, but it's worth it. Because now I finally get to seal the deal."

Loon glanced at him. He had always wondered why Meir trusted Lyor so much because he always felt something was off about the guy.

"Hey, Lyor. I see you got this under control. I'm gonna take this bitch to Hayward. A private jet is waiting for us there," said Phil.

His guys were tying Kim up, like a hog. The exact same way he did her parents.

The rope was cutting so tight she screamed. One of Phil's boys got irritated and punched her right in the face to shut her up, but knocked her out in the process.

"Ay!" Phil shouted. "Don't bruise her face. The fuck?"

A bullet flew from his gun and entered the guy's forehead.

That was for foregoing Ezra Kapon's request to have Kim unharmed.

Loon glanced at her. He hated himself for not being able to do anything. For not being able to keep his promise to her, that he would protect her.

"A'ight, man. What about my payment?" asked Lyor.

"I will wire it to you as soon as possible," Phil told him, exiting the house with his boys.

Lyor turned back to Loon. "So, where were we? Oh, right! I was about to shoot yo' ass." he picked up his gun. "Any last words, Loony?"

Loon nodded. "Yeah. Phil said not to kill me, remember?"

Lyor laughed starkly. "Fuck Phil! He don't run shit here. He could die next for all I care. I don't give a fuck."

He raised the gun to shoot him, but the rest of his crew burst in, interrupting them.

"What is it?" Lyor asked, annoyed.

Before they could answer, the door opened again, and Meir walked in. He stood by the door, with his hands in his pockets. "What's going on here, Lyor?" He asked.

"Er..." Lyor quickly stood up. "Look, Meir. I found him for you. He was just about to give me your money. Had to rough him up a bit," he said, chuckling nervously.

Meir smiled, nodding. "Is that so?" He asked, moving forward. "Cause I heard a different story."

"Oh yea?" said Lyor.

"Were you planning to kill me, Lyor?" Meir asked.

"Huh? What?" He shook his head. "No, no, no, no. No!"

Meir was still nodding and smiling. He really did know everything.

Lyor glanced at the boys, and they all looked down. They'd rather betray him than betray Meir. That much was clear.

Loon listened intently as Meir explained how he heard the whole conversation Lyor was having with him. He must have pocket-dialed him.

Lyor looked confused as hell, then scared.

Loon smirked at him. When Lyor slid the phone to him through the mail slot earlier, he had dialed Meir's number and set up Lyor to snitch on himself since he likes talking so much.

"Do you know what we do with traders like you?" Meir asked. He was now standing directly in front of Lyor.

Lyor's body began to shake. He was undoubtedly having a panic attack because he did know what they do with traders like him. Out of anxiety, he pulled the trigger and shot himself in the head from under his chin.

Loon shivered and cussed while Meir only looked away slightly.

"Well, that's it with that. Throw him out, boys" he said, offering his hand for Loon, who took it and got up from the floor.

"Thanks."

"Look, I'm sorry, man. I had no idea Lyor was doing all of that," said Meir. "All right? Let's just forget about it and work together. Gotta get the business back rolling. What do you say? I'd waive the debt of course."

"I appreciate it, Meir. Thank you so much blood, but I need your help with something at the moment and it's very urgent."

"Sure, what is it?"

Loon struggled to regain his composure. "Do you have a connection with someone that could help shut down the takeoff of a private jet?"

Meir tightened his lip for a moment. "Yeah, there is a guy. What airport is it and when is it taking off?"

Loon grinned. "Hayward Executive and I'd say it's taking off any moment now."

Meir and Loon drove to the airport in one of Meir's cars. Meir was on the phone, nodding slowly.

"Thanks, Leon. I owe you big time my friend." He gripped the wheel firmly, "Oh, and I've been hearing about your youngest boy. He's creating quite the buzz out there, huh?" A short pause and he nodded. "Yeah, okay. We'll talk soon."

After the call, Meir turned to Loon. "We should be good when we get to the airport."

They got to the airport and security tried to stop them at the gate. Loon shifted impatiently, but Meir assured him there'd be no issues. He rolled down his window, light glistening against it.

"Let us through, Leon King is an associate of mine," Meir said with confidence. The security guard turned to another guy who nodded.

"We were given a heads up to expect them, no questions asked. Let 'em through."

The gate arm rose up a second later, and they drove in.

There was only one jet there, and sure enough, Phil and his guys were seen boarding the jet with Kim.

"There they are," Loon said. Meir parked and Loon got out the car. "Philip!" He yelled.

Phil turned around, surprised to see him. "Take her inside," he said to the guys.

"Give me the girl!" yelled Loon again. He raised his gun and fired two warning shots in the air.

Kim was untied now and when she heard Loon's voice, she turned around and tried to run but one of the guys yet again grabbed her by the arm and lifted her off her feet, taking her up the staircase to the plane.

Phil smirked. "See, that's what..." he was interrupted as more cars began piling in. Several armed men got out and they all had their guns pointed at him. Phil frowned. He was outnumbered... again.

"Loon," he began. "You don't understand. You've got to let me get on that plane."

Loon shrugged. "Of course, you can, Phil. Just not with Kim. You can go to the Maldives for a vacation. I don't give a fuck. Just release the girl."

Phil raised his hands up. "Okay, okay. Here's a deal I think you are gonna like. 1ook if you let me walk away with her. Don't you have a fiancée to get back to?"

"I don't want your money, Phil. I just want Kim," Loon told him.

Meir snickered. He had been quiet all this time. "There is no way he'll harm her since he obviously wants her alive for something. We could just rush over and grab her, honestly."

Phil's brows furrowed. Meir was right. Before he could give the order for that, his phone rang. He brought it out and it was Ezra.

He quickly picked up the call, signaling for his guys to wait. "Hey, Ezra."

"Step aside, nephew."

"What?" Meir asked, confused.

"You heard me. Step aside," Ezra said. "That man works for me, and I need him to fulfill his duties."

Realization hit Meir as he put the pieces together. He was angry to find out his uncle was behind all of this. So, that was why he needed Lyor's contact and info. He turned to Loon and the boys. "I might have had a hand in all this," he said, without ending the call. "Yo, Ezra. This is really fucked up, unc, and I want nothing to do with it or you anymore."

There was a long pause before Ezra said, "Suit yourself," chuckling.

"You think I didn't know about all the extra money you were making and not kicking any up to me? I'm the boss, and you being family is the only thing that kept you alive all these years." He laughed again and mumbled something to someone. Meir couldn't make out what he said.

"Who were you talking to?" He asked.

"No one," said Ezra. "Just say hello to my sister for me."

Meir tilted his brows as if Ezra could see him. Ezra's

sister, his mother, had died 12 years ago of breast cancer. And what Ezra said could mean only one thing. Before he could tell that to Loon, a bullet went through his head and Meir fell to the ground, dead. Everyone was shocked to see that and had no idea where the shot came from. On the rooftop of a building across from the airport, the nozzle of a powerful sniping rifle glimmered, and the sniper gnashed his teeth and exhaled, eyes still on the scope, leather gloves crunching.

Phil tried to use that opportunity to run up the steps to the plane, but just when he was halfway up, the pilot stepped out and without hesitation, shot Phil twice in the head.

Kim screamed from inside the plane and that took Loon's attention. He quickly looked up, at Phil's dead body and the pilot who closed the door.

Almost immediately, the engines started.

"Fuck!" He cussed, running towards the plane. One of Meir's men stopped him, by grabbing his shoulders.

"Stay behind. We still don't know where that shot came from," the man said.

Loon struggled to break free, but the man held him tight. It was for his safety.

The plane headed off down the runway, and the man dragged Loon into one of the trucks. They all boarded the cars and sped off.

Loon had a blank look on his face as he stared at the plane's retreating figure. He couldn't figure out what he was feeling, it was like he didn't have a heart. He began punching the back of the seats and the car's window in anger. He knew the boys were right to fall back, but he had just lost Kim and he hated himself for that. He was quiet throughout the ride back to Oakland and his heart felt so heavy as if a stone was sitting atop it.

"There's a dead man in Israel," he announced emotionlessly, staring out the window.